Lulu Bell and the Christmas Elf

A Random House book
Published by Random House Australia Pty Ltd
Level 3, 100 Pacific Highway, North Sydney NSW 2060
www.randomhouse.com.au

First published by Random House Australia in 2014

Addresses for companies within the Random House Group can be found at www.randomhouse.com.au/offices

National Library of Australia
Cataloguing-in-Publication Entry

Author: Murrell, Belinda
Title: Lulu Bell and the Christmas elf/Belinda Murrell; illustrated by Serena Geddes
ISBN: 978 0 85798 503 3 (paperback)
Series: Murrell, Belinda. Lulu Bell; 9
Target audience: For primary school age
Subjects: Christmas – Juvenile fiction
Cats – Juvenile fiction
Other authors/contributors: Geddes, Serena
Dewey number: A823.4

Cover and internal illustrations by Serena Geddes
Cover design by Christabella Designs
Internal design and typesetting in 16/22 pt Bembo by Ingo Voss, Voss Designs, based on series design by Anna Warren, Warren Ventures
Printed in Australia by Griffin Press, an accredited ISO AS/NZS 14001:2004 Environmental Management System printer

Random House Australia uses papers that are natural, renewable and recyclable products and made from wood grown in sustainable forests. The logging and manufacturing processes are expected to conform to the environmental regulations of the country of origin.

Lulu Bell and the Christmas Elf

Belinda Murrell
Illustrated by Serena Geddes

RANDOM HOUSE AUSTRALIA

Lulu
Dad

Mum
Gus
Rosie

For Olivia and Jo, Amy and Roy, Lindy and Brett
in memory of a very special Australian Christmas

Chapter 1

The Tree

It was Saturday morning, a few days before Christmas. The Bell family was putting up the Christmas tree in the lounge room. Lulu Bell felt her tummy fizz with excitement. Today was going to be a very big day. There was so much to do!

Mum huffed as she and Dad hauled the tall pine tree upright. Mum stood back to check if it was straight. The top branch curled against the ceiling. The air was filled with the scent of pine resin from the tree and mangoes in the bowl on the table. It was the smell of Christmas.

'A little to the left,' said Mum, waving her hand.

Dad corrected the angle.

'Perfect,' Mum said.

Lulu and her little sister Rosie opened a cardboard box that was sitting on the floor. It was like a treasure chest filled with sparkling baubles. There were glass balls, silver stars, wooden animals, home-made paper chains and coloured lights.

'Who wants to put the first decoration on the tree?' asked Dad.

'Me, me, me,' shrieked Lulu, Rosie and their little brother Gus.

Mum smiled and covered her ears. 'Why don't we each choose one? Then we can all hang a decoration at the same time.'

Lulu peered into the box. Gus chose a tiny baby Jesus asleep in a nutshell. Rosie selected a gold heart. Lulu hesitated. Which ornament should she choose? Perched on top of the pile was a silver rocking horse.

Lulu held it up. 'Ready?' she asked.

Together they each hung a decoration on the tree. Then another and another. Soon the tree glowed and twinkled with a rainbow of colours and lights.

Pepper, the ginger cat, was fascinated. She sat back on her hind legs. With her front paw she batted a sparkly gold ball hanging from one of the lower branches. The ball flew through the air and rolled across the floor.

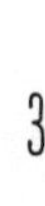

‘Oh, no you don’t, Pepper,’ scolded Lulu. She scooped Pepper up and carried her from the room. ‘I know you. You’ll be up to all sorts of mischief if I let you stay in there.’

Pepper purred and rubbed her head against Lulu’s chin. Lulu purred back and cuddled her. She put Pepper down on the kitchen floor and closed the door.

Rosie was crawling under the couch to rescue the ball.

‘I think we should put the best ornaments up high,’ suggested Mum. ‘I don’t want the cats smashing any of them.’

Dad hung the gold ball safely near the top.

At last there was just one special ornament left in the bottom of the box. It was a white-and-gold angel on a scarlet

ribbon. The three children gathered around expectantly.

'This year I think it's Rosie's turn,' said Mum. 'Come on, honey bun.'

Rosie picked the angel out of the box with gentle hands. Her face shone with excitement. Dad lifted her high, high into the air. Rosie looked like she was flying. She stretched up and popped the angel on top of the tree. Dad helped Rosie to loop the ribbon securely to a branch.

'There,' said Mum. 'It's finished.'

Lulu examined the tree. She smiled with satisfaction.

'The tree looks amazing,' said Lulu. 'I can't wait for Christmas.'

'Do you think Santa will bring us lots of presents?' asked Rosie.

'Want presents now,' said Gus. He looked up at his big sisters hopefully. 'Want Santa come now.'

Lulu put her hand on her hip. 'Santa doesn't come for another week, Gus. First we have the Christmas concert and we

finish school. Then there's the Christmas Eve party and *then* Santa comes.'

'We haven't even written our letters to Santa yet,' said Rosie. 'I can't make up my mind what to ask for. A ballerina doll? Or maybe a tutu?'

'A piggy,' said Gus.

Mum threw her arms up in the air. She kissed Gus on top of his head.

'Definitely no pigs,' said Mum. 'Let's get a wriggle on. We have lots to do today. First we'll bake shortbread for the teachers.' She ticked the list off on her fingers. 'Then make Christmas decorations and props for the school concert on Monday. *And* we have to finish making the costumes.'

'Lucky we have lots of helpers coming over for the working bee,' said Lulu.

Dad looked at everyone in horror. He didn't enjoy craft as much as the rest of the family. 'I'd *love* to help but I think it's time I went to work.'

He hurried off next door. Lulu's dad was a vet. The family lived in a rambling old house right behind the Shelly Beach Vet Hospital. Saturday mornings were always busy with lots of animal patients to see.

Usually Lulu loved to help there. But not today. This Saturday morning Lulu was very excited about helping Mum instead.

Mum picked up the empty cardboard box. She tucked it under her arm. 'Let's get cracking, honey buns.'

Chapter 2

Preparations

Soon the kitchen was filled with delicious smells. The spicy scent of nutmeg and cinnamon from the apple sauce. The buttery sweetness of choc-chunk shortbread baking.

Rosie and Gus were cutting out more dough with star-shaped biscuit cutters. Jessie, the smiley dog, sniffed around the floor searching for crumbs.

Lulu juiced a pile of lemons. She poured the juice into a saucepan with butter and sugar.

Mum stirred the mixture on the stovetop until it was hot and thick. Then she poured the syrupy lemon butter into several clean jars. The golden liquid glowed and steamed in the sunlight.

'Nearly done,' said Mum.

'I can't wait to give our present to Miss Martin,' said Rosie. 'She will love it.'

Miss Martin was Rosie's year one teacher. For Christmas they would give each of their teachers a thank-you present of home-made goodies. There would be jars of apple sauce and lemon butter, plus home-made jam and choc-chunk shortbread.

'So will Miss Baxter,' said Lulu. 'She deserves a delicious present. She has been the best teacher.'

'I don't *want* a new teacher next year,' said Rosie. Her voice wobbled. 'I wish I

could have Miss Martin forever and ever.'

Mum smoothed Rosie's hair back from her forehead. 'You'll have a lovely new teacher next year, honey bun,' said Mum. 'Won't she, Lulu?'

Lulu nodded. 'All the teachers are nice, Rosie. You'll see.'

Rosie stuck out her lip and shook her head.

When the cooking was finished, Mum cleaned up.

Lulu and Rosie sat at the kitchen table making Christmas star bunting. They cut out stars from brown cardboard recycled from old boxes. Then the girls painted each star with a wash of purple watercolour.

Gus was sitting on the floor and sticking glitter on his star. There seemed to be more glitter on the floor than on

the cardboard. Jessie tried to lick it up. She ended up with a sparkly blue muzzle.

Lulu used the hole puncher to cut holes in the stars. Then she strung the stars on a long piece of string.

'Look, Mum,' said Lulu. 'What do you think?'

Lulu and Rosie held up one end of the string each. The stars fluttered in the breeze from the open door.

'Good work, honey buns,' said Mum. 'That will look gorgeous on the tree for the concert.'

At ten o'clock, Lulu's best friend Molly came over to help. She arrived with her brother Sam and mother Tien. Molly's mum was good at sewing and often helped to make costumes for the school.

Mum and Tien started cutting up old white sheets. They were making angel dresses for all the kids in Rosie's class.

Rosie was the model. She wore a halo of gold tinsel on her hair and gold tinsel around her waist. Lulu and Molly made more tinsel haloes and belts.

Sam and Gus practised forward rolls in the kitchen. As usual, Gus was wearing his favourite superhero outfit.

'I wonder where Roy is?' asked Mum. 'He said he'd come over early to help with the props. He's usually so punctual.'

Roy was the father of Lulu's friends Olivia and Josephine. They were twins in Lulu's class. Olivia was the oldest by just a few minutes. She was a beautiful singer, while Jo was a talented piano player. They would be performing a duet together at the Christmas concert.

'Perhaps something came up,' suggested Tien. 'Everyone is busy at the end of the year. He should be here soon.'

Tien and Mum finished the angel dresses and started on the elf costumes for Lulu's class. Mum cut out the green material while Tien stitched pieces together on the sewing machine.

'Come and try this on for me please, honey bun,' said Mum. 'I want to see how it looks.'

Lulu changed into her elf costume. She wore a red-and-white striped t-shirt with stripy tights. Over the top she wore a green tunic. On her feet were green curly-toed slippers with golden bells.

Mum popped a red elf hat on her head. 'Perfect,' she said.

Gus looked at Lulu in her costume. He pulled a silly face. 'Lulu funny. Lulu Christmas elf.'

Lulu laughed. 'Not as funny as you, Gus.'

Rosie skipped across the kitchen. Her halo slipped over one ear.

'I can't wait for the school concert,' said Rosie. 'It will be so much fun.'

The two dogs were lying on their beds in the corner. Suddenly Asha

woofed and ran to the door. She wagged her tail and sniffed. A moment later someone knocked.

'That must be Roy and the girls,' said Mum.

Lulu ran to open the door. The bells on her slippers jingled and tinkled.

It was Olivia and Jo with their dad. Although the girls were twins, they were not alike. Olivia had dark hair and dark eyes, like her mum. Jo had fair hair and blue eyes. Lulu smiled at the girls.

But something was wrong.

Usually Olivia had a happy, smiling face with two deep dimples in her cheeks. Not today.

'Sorry we're late,' said Roy. He spoke with a soft Dutch accent. He was a tall man, with dimples just like Olivia's. 'We had a problem at home.'

Roy came in, carrying a pile of cardboard boxes and a big roll of canvas.

'Never mind,' said Mum, waving her hand. 'We're making good progress.'

Roy put the boxes on the floor. 'I'll get to work covering these boxes,' he said. 'Then I have some last-minute touch-ups to our sleigh.'

The parents chatted as they set to work. The girls stood near the door. Molly came to join them.

'Is everything all right?' asked Lulu. 'You both look so worried.'

Jo stared at the ground as though she was trying hard not to cry.

Olivia sighed. 'Bonnie is missing,' she said. 'We've looked everywhere for her.'

Bonnie was the girls' fluffy tri-colour cat. She sometimes came for check-ups at

the vet hospital. Lulu knew that the girls adored her.

'Oh no,' said Lulu. 'I'm so sorry. How long has she been gone?'

'Since yesterday morning,' said Olivia.

'We thought Bonnie would come for dinner last night,' said Jo. 'We called and called.'

'Mum said not to worry,' said Olivia. 'She thought Bonnie would probably be home for breakfast. But she wasn't. We've searched everywhere.'

Jo wiped her eyes. Lulu gave her a hug.

'She's been missing so long,' said Olivia. 'We just don't know what to do.'

'We need to make a plan to find her,' said Lulu. 'Come with me.'

Chapter 3

A Plan

Lulu led the girls into her bedroom. They all sat on the rug.

Lulu pushed one honey-coloured plait behind her ear and started to speak. 'First, we need to let people know that Bonnie is missing. That way, if anyone finds her they will know who to call.'

'We could put an ad in the newspaper,' said Olivia.

'Yes,' said Jo. 'And we could make an announcement in assembly at school.'

'Fantastic,' said Lulu. She jumped up and fetched the art box from the corner.

'We should make some posters too. We can stick them up in the vet hospital and on the power poles near your house.'

'That's a great idea,' said Jo. 'We could put some up at the bus stop too.'

'And the noticeboards at the shops,' said Molly.

Olivia smiled. Her dimples were back. 'Let's get to work,' she said.

Jo took a piece of paper from the box. She sketched out a rough poster. 'What do you think?'

The girls read the wording. 'Add in that she's friendly,' suggested Olivia.

'Don't forget to say when she disappeared,' said Molly.

'And that if someone finds her they can bring her to Shelly Beach Vet Hospital,' added Lulu.

Jo made the changes. When they were happy with the wording, the girls started making copies of the poster.

When the girls had made a big pile of posters, Lulu led the way next door. The girls pushed through the green door into the vet hospital.

Kylie the vet nurse sat at the reception desk. She was talking to a client with a cockatiel perched on his shoulder. The bird shrieked at them. He raised his crest of feathers high.

'Hello, girls,' said Kylie, smiling at them. 'I like your elf costume, Lulu. It's very Christmassy.'

'Thanks, Kylie,' said Lulu. 'It's for our school concert.'

'Oh, I'm looking forward to it,' said Kylie. She turned to Olivia and Jo. 'I hear you two are giving a special performance?'

The girls nodded. 'We're the very last act,' said Jo.

Kylie noticed the pile of posters that Olivia carried. 'What are you girls up to?' she asked.

'We made some posters to put up,' said Lulu. 'Bonnie is missing.'

Kylie frowned. 'That's terrible news,' she said. 'I'm so sorry. But putting up posters is a great idea. I'm sure she'll be found really soon.'

Kylie handed Lulu some sticky tape.

Olivia and Jo stuck a poster in the window. Molly and Lulu put one on the front of the reception desk.

'Now we need to put posters around the neighbourhood,' said Lulu.

'Let's ask Dad if he can take us,' said Olivia. 'Would you and Molly like to come too?'

'Sure,' said Molly and Lulu together.

The girls went back to the house. The parents were still working hard. Mum was pinning material. Tien was sewing a tunic. Roy was covering empty cardboard boxes in silver paper. These would be props to decorate the stage.

'Dad,' called Olivia. 'We made some posters to let people know that Bonnie is missing.'

'What a great idea, *meisje*,' said Roy. Roy often called the girls *meisje*. It was a Dutch word that meant 'little girl'.

'We want to stick them up on power poles and on noticeboards,' added Jo.

'Could you take us?'

'Of course,' said Roy. 'Let me finish wrapping this box. It's the last one.'

Roy and the four girls walked around the streets. They stuck posters on power poles, noticeboards and bus shelters. Every time they met someone, they asked if they had seen a lost tri-colour cat. But no-one had.

Olivia and Jo stuck the last poster up on the noticeboard outside the bakery.

'I hope this works,' said Jo. 'I hope someone rings today.'

'I don't know what we'll do if we can't find Bonnie,' said Olivia. 'It would be the saddest Christmas ever.'

Roy walked the girls back to Lulu's house. Lulu gave both twins a big hug to give them courage. Inside, Mum and Tien had just finished the last elf costume.

Rosie jumped up, waving a sheet of paper. 'Come *on*, Lulu. I've been waiting for you for ages. We need to write our letters to Santa. I know *exactly* what to ask for.'

Lulu smiled at Rosie. 'A new tutu?'

'No,' said Rosie. 'I've thought of something much better than that.'

Molly, Sam and Tien went home. Lulu, Rosie and Gus sat down at the kitchen bench to write their letters to Santa. All three of them had something very special to ask for.

Dear Santa

I hope you are well. You must be very busy at this time of year.

Santa, I have a very big favour to ask. Instead of bringing us presents, do you think you could please find my friends' cat Bonnie? She is a lovely cat and we are all very worried about her. If you brought Bonnie back, that would make us all so happy.

Thank you so much. Merry Christmas.

Love
Lulu Bell

P.S. I hope the reindeer like the carrots. We made you some choc-chunk shortbread, plus some extra to take home to Mrs Claus.

dear SAntA

my nAMe is Rosie Bell. All i WAnt For christMAS is miss mArtin. She is My teACher At Shelly BeACh SChool. She is so niCe. i Don't WAnt A new teACher next yeAr.

ThAnk you

Rosie

p.S. you Don't neeD to bring miss mArtin Down the ChiMney.

Dear Santa

This letter is from my little brother Gus. He has mostly been good, although sometimes he can be naughty. But he's only three.

Gus says he would really like a piglet for Christmas. He loves pigs.

I don't think Mum would like a piglet in the back garden. So if that's too hard, maybe Gus would love a wooden sword.

Thanks so much.
Lulu (writing for Gus)

P.S. Gus would like it if you brought Bonnie back too.

Chapter 4

Where Are The Twins?

Monday was a busy and exciting day. It was the last day of school before the holidays. It was also the day of the Christmas concert.

Dad and Roy had set up a Christmas tree in the playground next to the stage. The kids decorated it with hand-made ornaments. Lulu and Rosie hung up their star bunting. The stage was decorated with piles of the giant fake presents that Roy had wrapped.

Underneath the tree were lots of real presents that the students had donated. The presents would be given to children who weren't quite as lucky as the kids at Shelly Beach School. Lulu and Rosie had chosen a pile of books to give away.

During the day, all the classes rehearsed their acts one last time. The kids helped set up chairs for the parents and grandparents in the playground.

At last it was time for the concert. It was a beautiful summer afternoon. The sun shone brightly. The sky was a deep blue with wisps of white cloud. A breeze from the ocean kept the playground cool.

In the afternoon, all the kids dressed in their costumes. Lulu and Molly peered out of their classroom window.

'Look,' said Lulu. 'Everyone is arriving.'

‘There’s your mum and dad,’ said Molly. ‘And Gus.’

Mum had her big camera slung around her neck. Gus was dressed in a Christmas elf costume just like Lulu’s.

‘And Nanna and Gumpa,’ added Lulu. She pointed at her grandparents as they sat down in the front row.

Tien and Kylie walked through the gate together. Then came Olivia and Jo's mum and dad, their grandparents Ninny and Pa, and their great-grandmother Peorie.

All the families were super-excited. They chatted and laughed as they found their seats.

Inside the classroom, Miss Baxter was handing out the elf hats. She turned to Lulu and Molly with a frown.

'Have you girls seen Olivia and Jo?' asked Miss Baxter. 'They should be here by now.'

Lulu looked around the room. All of the other students were there. They were giggling and joking as they tried on their hats.

'I saw them a while ago,' replied Lulu. 'They were already dressed.'

Miss Baxter looked worried. 'Could you look for them for me, please, girls? I know they're sad today because Bonnie is missing. I hope everything is all right.'

Lulu nodded. The bell on her elf hat jingled.

'Of course, Miss Baxter,' said Molly.

'We'll be as fast as we can,' added Lulu.

Molly and Lulu raced out of the classroom. 'Where do you think they could be?' asked Molly.

'Let's start by checking all the classrooms on this level,' suggested Lulu. 'Maybe they are visiting the other year three class.'

Every classroom was filled with excited children in different costumes. There were reindeer, Christmas trees, fairies, nutcracker soldiers and animals. But there was no sign of the twins.

Molly and Lulu kept searching in the bathrooms, the library and the computer lab.

At last they checked in the art room. As Molly pushed open the door, Lulu could hear a funny noise coming from inside. It sounded like crying.

Olivia and Jo sat huddled together under the window.

'What's wrong?' asked Molly. She ran over to the girls.

Jo looked up, her eyes red from crying. Olivia wiped her face with a tissue.

Lulu thought it was awful to see the girls so upset. They were usually so happy and cheerful.

'There's still no sign of Bonnie,' said Olivia. 'We put up all those posters and no-one has called.'

'Something terrible must have happened to her,' said Jo.

Lulu gave each of the girls a hug.

'I know you're worried,' said Lulu. 'But Miss Baxter sent us to find you. The concert is starting any minute. You need to come and join the class.'

Olivia and Jo shook their heads.

'I couldn't possibly sing when I feel so bad,' said Olivia.

'Or play the piano,' added Jo.

'We'd spoil the concert,' said Olivia.

Molly looked worried. 'But your performance is beautiful,' she said. 'I saw you rehearse it last week.'

Olivia gave Molly a watery smile.

'Everyone is looking forward to it,'

said Lulu. 'You are the stars of the show.'

Jo shook her head. She sniffled and blew her nose. Molly sat down next to Jo and put her arm around her shoulder.

Lulu thought quickly. How could she help the girls feel better? She smiled at the twins.

'How long has Bonnie been missing?' she asked.

Jo rubbed her eyes. 'Four days. Since Friday.'

Lulu nodded. 'That's not so bad. We've had cats brought into the vet hospital that have been missing for weeks. We always find their owners.'

Olivia and Jo looked at each other hopefully.

Lulu picked up a water bottle that was sitting on a desk. She gave a cheeky smile.

‘Anyway,’ said Lulu, ‘it doesn’t matter. If you can’t perform, Molly and I will do it for you.’

Olivia and Jo stared at Lulu in surprise.

‘What do you mean?’ asked Jo.

Lulu struck a pose. She held the water bottle as though it were a microphone.

'O, holy night!' sang Lulu. She wiggled her hips and shook her head from side to side. She pointed at the two girls. *'The stars are brightly shining.'*

Molly laughed. Olivia and Jo giggled at Lulu's antics. Lulu had a nice voice but it wasn't deep and strong like Olivia's.

'Your mum and dad are here,' said Lulu. 'And your ninny and pa, and even your great-grandmother. But I'm sure they wouldn't mind if Molly and I sang instead.'

'I can't play the piano,' said Molly. 'But I could play the air guitar.'

She jumped around and strummed an imaginary guitar like a rock star. Lulu banged on the desk like a drum. The noise was terrible.

Everyone laughed. Olivia's dimples came back.

Jo shook her head. 'Ninny is so looking forward to it,' she said.

'And Pa,' added Olivia.

'And your dad helped make all the sets,' Lulu reminded them. 'He would be so sad if he didn't get to see you perform.'

The twins hesitated.

'Perhaps Molly and I could just *help* you,' suggested Lulu. 'We could play the air guitar – or we could stick to turning cartwheels.'

The twins nodded and jumped to their feet.

'Let's go,' said Olivia and Jo together.

Chapter 5

The Christmas Spectacular

All the other children were in the playground. They were sitting cross-legged in their class groups. The first act had already begun.

Miss Baxter smiled when she saw Lulu, Molly, Olivia and Jo hurrying across the playground. They sat down with the class.

'Thanks, girls,' she whispered. 'I was worried that we had lost our star performers.'

'We were just working on a little surprise,' Lulu whispered back.

Every class at Shelly Beach School performed in the concert. The children sang songs, danced and played music. There were Christmas carols, poetry recitals and a nativity play. Sam's kindy class danced. All the kids were dressed as reindeer. Sam wore a bright red plastic nose.

Rosie's year one class sang a Christmas carol. They were all dressed in the angel costumes that Mum and Tien had made.

Lulu felt jumpy with nerves. It was time for her class to line up at the back of the stage. Roy grinned at the girls as he slipped past them. He was on his way to get changed. He would be making a special guest appearance in the concert.

The next act finished.

'Come on, everyone,' said Miss Baxter. 'It's our turn.'

Lulu grinned at Molly, then at Olivia and Jo.

On the stage, a roll of canvas dropped down as a back-drop. Mum and Roy had painted a huge white horse and an old-fashioned sleigh onto it.

'I would like to introduce the 3B elves performing "Jingle Bells",' announced Miss Baxter.

The music began. The whole class ran onto the stage. Lulu could see her family sitting in the audience. Gus stood up on his chair and waved. Mum had the camera aimed and ready. Nanna and Gumpa blew kisses.

The elves began their dance – spinning and turning, jumping and swooping.

Then Roy strode out on stage, wearing a long white beard. His blue eyes twinkled. He was dressed as Santa Claus, with a big pillow stuffed down his front.

All the kids cheered. Santa Claus danced around, surrounded by elves.

The elves danced and sang their hearts out. Lulu and Molly turned cartwheels. At last it was finished.

Everyone bowed, then ran off the stage.

The parents and grandparents clapped and cheered. Gus danced up and down on his chair. Roy sat back in the audience, right in the front.

Miss Baxter took the microphone again. 'We are nearly at the end of our Christmas concert,' she said. 'I would now like to introduce some very talented performers. Here are the twins Olivia and Jo from year three.'

The twins ran onto the stage. They had quickly changed from their elf outfits. Now they wore long tutus made of tulle. Olivia's was turquoise with a white ribbon around her waist, while Jo's was white with a turquoise ribbon.

Lulu gave the twins a thumbs-up sign. The girls smiled.

Jo took a seat at the piano. A hush fell over the audience. Jo started playing.

Olivia stood at the microphone. She began to sing 'O Holy Night'. Her voice was strong and clear.

Lulu and Molly ran onto the stage behind the twins. They danced and swayed. Then Lulu realised there was another dancer on the stage. Gus had run up to join them. He pranced and spun in his little elf suit. Gus waved to the crowd.

'A thrill of hope,' sang Olivia. She pointed towards all the mums and dads, grandmothers and grandfathers in the audience. *'The weary world rejoices. For yonder breaks a new and glorious morn.'*

As Olivia sang the final chorus, Molly and Lulu flipped into their cartwheels. They spun and turned across the front of the stage.

The audience clapped and clapped. Parents mopped their eyes. Miss Baxter beamed. Fathers cheered. But the loudest cheers of all came from Dad and Roy standing up in the front row.

Olivia and Jo stood up and bowed. Then Olivia grabbed Lulu by the hand, and Jo grabbed Molly and Gus by the hands. They dragged them forward to the front of the stage. All four girls and Gus bowed together and waved.

'Thanks, Lulu,' whispered Olivia. 'I don't think we could have performed if you and Molly hadn't cheered us up.'

'You were both wonderful,' said Lulu. 'The concert wouldn't have been the same without your song.'

Lulu squeezed Olivia's hand. 'Don't be sad about Bonnie. I'm sure someone will find her soon.'

Miss Baxter came on stage and beckoned to all the students. They came running.

For the very last act all the children in the whole school gathered in front of the stage. They sang one final song at the tops of their voices.

'*We* wish *you a merry Christmas and a Happy New* Year.'

Chapter 6

The Phone Call

The Bell family had just arrived home from the Christmas concert. Everyone was happy and tired. Rosie was singing Christmas carols and spinning around the kitchen. Gus was sleepy. He climbed into Mum's lap and snuggled up.

Dad opened the back door to let the dogs inside. It was still warm and sunny outside – a beautiful summer evening. Pepper the ginger cat came running in from the lounge room. Lulu scooped her up and stroked her long, silky fur.

Lulu purred at Pepper. Pepper responded with a deep, throaty rumble.

'I'm glad Pepper and Pickles haven't gone missing,' said Lulu. She started to make the cats' dinner.

'Pepper loves her dinner too much to go wandering off,' said Mum. She looked down at the boy on her lap. 'Just like you, Gus.'

Suddenly a phone rang in the kitchen. It was the phone that rang after the vet hospital had closed for the day.

Dad answered it. 'Shelly Beach Vet Hospital. Dr Bell speaking. Can I help you?'

Dad listened as the caller explained.

‘I’ll come right away,’ he said. ‘What’s your address?’ Dad scrawled the details down on a piece of paper. ‘Thanks. I’ll be there as soon as I can.’

Dad turned to the family. ‘A lady just rang to say that she heard a cat meowing under her house. She said it won’t come out and it seems to be in distress.’

Lulu’s face lit up. ‘Do you think it could be Bonnie?’

‘I don’t know,’ said Dad. ‘She lives quite a few streets away from Olivia and Jo’s house. But there’s only one way to find out. Would you like to come with me?’

‘Yes, please,’ replied Lulu.

Dad and Lulu drove to the far side of Shelly Beach. Dad parked the station wagon and collected a carry cage from the back. He and Lulu walked to the front door and rang the bell.

An older woman answered. She had a kind, crinkly face. 'Hello, Dr Bell,' she said. 'Thanks for coming.'

'Hello, Mrs Russell,' said Dad. 'This is my daughter Lulu.'

Mrs Russell smiled at Lulu.

'Let's see if you have more luck coaxing the poor cat out from under my house,' Mrs Russell said. 'I've called and called but it won't come.'

She led the way around the back. It was a timber house that was raised slightly above the ground. The gap was too small for a person to crawl into. But it was just big enough for a small animal like a cat.

'I heard it meowing on and off over the weekend,' explained Mrs Russell. 'I've coaxed and cajoled, and left out food and milk. I've tried everything. Then I saw a poster up at the shops about a missing cat, so I rang you.'

'Thank you, Mrs Russell,' said Dad. 'Let's see if we can persuade this cat to come out.'

Lulu and her dad listened carefully. They couldn't hear anything but the sound of cars on the road and the breeze rustling the leaves on the trees.

'Here, pussa, pussa,' called Dad. 'Here, pussa.'

They listened again. Lulu thought she heard a faint whimper.

'I heard something,' whispered Lulu.

'Here, pussa. Here, Bonnie.' Dad called again and again. There was no sign of a cat.

Lulu lay on her tummy on the lawn. She peered into the shadows under the house. It was too hard to see anything. Lulu wondered if it really was Bonnie hiding under the house. She imagined her frightened and possibly hurt.

Lulu had been to visit Olivia and Jo's house many times. She had often cuddled

and stroked Bonnie. She used to talk to Bonnie just like she talked to her own cats. Lulu had an idea.

'Meow,' called Lulu softly. '*Meow*, Bonnie.'

There was no reply. Lulu tried again. *'Meow.'*

'Mew,' came a faint reply.

Lulu wriggled closer to the gap under the house. *'Meow.'*

Lulu meowed and meowed patiently. Dad and Mrs Russell sat on some outdoor chairs and waited.

Another whimper came from under the house but this time it sounded closer. Lulu put her hand in the gap under the house. She called again.

Gradually Lulu's eyes adjusted to the dimness under the house. At last she saw something move.

Could it be a cat? Could it be Bonnie?

Slowly, the shadow crawled forward. At last Lulu could reach it with her fingertips. She grasped the animal and hauled it out.

It was a filthy, bedraggled and very skinny cat. Its coat was black and white and orange. The fur was matted with dried grass and dust. The cat blinked at Lulu with huge green eyes. The pupils were wide and black.

'Bonnie!' cried Lulu.

The cat panted, struggling for breath.

Dad dashed over. 'Great work, Lulu.'

'Is she all right?' asked Mrs Russell.

Dad frowned as he examined the limp cat. 'Her hind legs aren't working,' he said. 'She's very weak. I think she has tick poisoning.'

Lulu felt a cold shiver run up her spine. 'Poor Bonnie,' she said.

'We need to get back to the vet hospital as quickly as possible,' Dad said.

He wrapped Bonnie in a towel and gently placed her in the carry cage. They said their goodbyes and thank-yous to Mrs Russell. Dad put the cage in the back of the car.

Lulu felt very worried. She knew that paralysis ticks were dangerous for cats and dogs. Every summer lots of animals came into the vet hospital for treatment.

Had they found Bonnie in time?

Chapter 7

Treatment

Back at the vet hospital, Dad carried Bonnie straight into one of the consulting rooms. He put her on the table.

'Can you help me hold her, please, sweetie?' asked Dad.

Lulu stood on the opposite side of the table and held Bonnie still. Lulu's tummy was filled with butterflies.

Dad pulled on a pair of gloves and gave Bonnie a quick injection to sedate her.

He began running his fingertips through Bonnie's fur. After a minute of careful searching, he paused.

'Got it,' he said. There was a swollen grey tick buried in the skin on the back of Bonnie's neck. Dad took a pair of tweezers from the instrument tray. He used the tweezers to carefully lever the tick away from the skin. He dropped the tick into a stainless steel dish.

Lulu sighed with relief. Dad kept searching until he was sure there were no more ticks.

'Will she be all right?' asked Lulu.

Dad looked worried. 'It looks like that tick had been there for quite a few days. She's having trouble breathing.'

He rummaged in the cupboard and pulled out a bottle of serum. He gave Bonnie another injection. 'This anti-toxin should fight the tick poison.'

Bonnie stared at Lulu with big green eyes. The cat panted and wheezed.

Lulu and Dad worked together to make Bonnie more comfortable. Lulu combed the twigs and dirt out of her fur. Dad put her on an intravenous drip to give her some fluid. Then he propped Bonnie up on a rolled-up towel. That would make it easier for her to breathe.

Dad rang Roy to tell him that Bonnie was found safe.

A few minutes later, Olivia and Jo burst through the door. Their parents Roy and Amy came behind.

'Where is she?' asked Jo.

'Is she all right?' asked Olivia.

'Oh, she's so skinny,' said Jo.

Bonnie meowed pitifully. The girls stroked her head. The twins were torn between happiness that Bonnie was found, and worry that she was so sick. Dad explained the treatment he had given her.

'When will we know whether Bonnie is out of danger?' asked Roy.

'We should know more in the next twenty-four hours,' said Dad. 'But in the meantime, Bonnie will be having a sleepover at the vet hospital for a couple

of days. I need to keep a very close eye on her.'

'Will Bonnie be better in time for Christmas?' asked Olivia.

Lulu grinned at Olivia and Jo.

'Of course she will,' said Lulu. 'Isn't she being looked after by the best vet in the world?'

Chapter 8

Bonnie Goes Home

Lulu was right.

On the day before Christmas, Lulu went next door to check on Bonnie. It was very busy at the vet hospital. Lots of clients were getting pets checked before the holidays. Other pets were being picked up.

In the hospital ward, Bonnie was curled up in a basket in her cage. When she saw Lulu she stood up slowly.

Bonnie rubbed her face against Lulu's hand and purred.

'Oh, Bonnie. You're up and walking,' cried Lulu. 'You're getting better.'

Just then Dad came in with a carry cage.

'Perfect timing, Lulu,' said Dad. 'Olivia and Jo are here to pick up Bonnie. Why don't you come in and see them?'

'I'd love to,' said Lulu.

Dad scooped Bonnie up and popped her in the carry cage. Lulu followed Dad into the consulting room. The whole family was already waiting in there. The twins were bursting with delight.

'Here she is,' said Dad. He lifted Bonnie out of the carry cage and put her on the examination table. 'Still a little wobbly but definitely on the mend.'

Olivia and Jo beamed. They cuddled and stroked Bonnie. Bonnie purred with pleasure.

'You'll need to keep her quiet for the next few days,' said Dad. 'She needs lots of rest and nourishing food.'

Roy nodded. 'That's really wonderful news.'

Olivia turned to Lulu. 'We've brought you a little present, Lulu,' she said.

'To thank you for coaxing Bonnie out,' added Jo.

Roy was carrying a box wrapped in coloured paper. He handed it to Lulu with a smile. 'Part of it is for your dad as well,' he said. 'We are so grateful to you both.'

Lulu loved getting presents. She carefully opened the box. Inside were two smaller packages. One was a cellophane bag full of home-made Christmas biscuits.

'They're *Kerstkransjes*,' said Roy.

'Dutch Christmas wreath biscuits,' said Jo. 'You hang them on the Christmas tree by the ribbon.'

'Then you eat them on Christmas Day,' added Olivia. 'They're delicious.'

Each round biscuit had a hole in the middle. A length of red ribbon was looped through the hole. The biscuits were decorated with chocolate and nuts.

They looked very pretty.

'Thank you,' said Lulu. 'I'll hang them up as soon as I go home.'

She tore the tissue paper off the last present. It was a pair of red wooden clogs. The toes were turned up just like Lulu's elf slippers. Lulu lifted one of the shoes out of the box.

'A present from Holland,' said Jo.

'We call them *klompen*,' said Roy. 'In Holland the children put their *klompen* out filled with hay or carrots for *Sinterklaas*'s big white horse.'

'*Sinterklaas* is the Dutch name for Santa Claus,' Olivia explained. 'If the children have been good, *Sinterklaas* fills the clogs with lollies. We thought you might like them.'

Lulu smiled at the girls. 'Thanks. They're beautiful.'

Lulu tried the clogs on her feet. They fit perfectly. She did a little jig to make the clogs clomp.

'Come on, girls,' said Roy. 'Let's get Bonnie home.'

He turned to Lulu and Dr Bell. His face dimpled with a smile. '*Vrolijke Kerstmis,*' said Roy.

'Merry Christmas,' replied Dad.

Chapter 9

Beach Party

As soon as Dad finished work, it was time for more Christmas celebrations. Every year the families of Shelly Beach had a Christmas Eve party at the beach.

The sun glowed golden in the late afternoon. It sparkled and glimmered on the blue sea. Yachts with white sails danced on the gentle swell. A pink-beaked pelican swooped and landed on a weathered wharf pylon.

The Bell children jumped out of the car. They chattered with excitement. All three kids were already dressed in swimming costumes, rash vests and sun hats. Gus carried a big red ball. Rosie carried a bucket and spade. Lulu carried the cricket set and her boogie board.

They ran down to the sand. Mum and Dad followed with the picnic basket and beach chairs.

Lots of their friends were already there. Molly was paddling in the water with Tien and Sam.

Lauren was building a sandcastle with her parents and brother. Some of the teachers from school were chatting, including Miss Baxter, Miss Donaldson and Miss Martin. Jo and Olivia arrived with Roy and Amy.

The kids raced into the water, dragging their boogie boards. They jumped and splashed and swam and surfed. Dad set up the cricket stumps and organised a huge game of cricket. Everyone played and laughed. They sang Christmas carols.

Molly, Olivia and Jo made up a new Christmas carol. It went like this:

Lulu Bell, Lulu Bell,
Lulu all the way.
Oh, what fun it is to play
With Lulu Bell today – hey!

Lulu laughed and clapped.

After the games, the parents set up a delicious picnic to share. There were bread rolls with roast chicken and salad. Tien had made rice paper rolls and prawn dumplings. Amy had baked an apple tart.

Lulu and Rosie gave their presents to their teachers. Each box held jars of lemon butter, jam and apple sauce, with bags of shortbread and a special card painted by the girls.

'How wonderful, Rosie! Thank you,' said Miss Martin. 'This all looks so delicious. And I love your painting.'

'I wrote a special letter to Santa,' said Rosie. 'I asked him if I could have *you* for Christmas.'

Miss Martin laughed. 'Thank you, Rosie. I am very flattered that you want me for Christmas.'

Lulu sighed. 'Rosie is sad that she won't have you as a teacher next year.'

Miss Martin crouched down next to Rosie. 'I'm sad that I won't have you in my class next year too, Rosie. I'll miss you. But you've grown up so much this year. You're doing so well that you're truly ready for year two.'

Rosie nodded slowly.

'And you can visit me in my classroom any time you want to,' added

Miss Martin. 'You could help me with the new year one students. Some of them will be very nervous coming into my big year one class.'

Rosie giggled. 'No-one would be nervous coming into *your* class.'

Miss Martin grinned. 'You know I can be *very* scary.'

The sun began to set in the west. It streaked the sky with a wash of crimson and gold.

Mum hugged Lulu close as they admired the view. 'Isn't it beautiful? It's Christmas Eve,' she whispered. 'Time to go home and hang up the stockings.'

Lulu jumped up and down. 'Mum, do I have time to write a new letter to Santa?'

Mum laughed. 'Yes, honey bun.'

'Me too,' said Rosie.

Everyone was sandy and salty and tired. They packed the car and drove home. All the houses were decorated with Christmas lights. It looked like fairyland.

Chapter 10

Christmas Eve

At home it was time for the final Christmas preparations. The children changed into their pyjamas and cleaned their teeth. They wrote their new letters to Santa. Then the whole family gathered in the lounge room.

'First, we'll hang up the stockings,' said Mum. Lulu's nanna had made them each a red stocking. Their names were sewn on in cloth letters. Mum handed them out.

Lulu, Gus and Rosie hung their stockings on the mantelpiece. Dad helped Gus to hang his because he was not quite tall enough to reach.

'Now I think we should put out a little snack for Santa, to say thank you for bringing presents,' suggested Mum.

'And a little something for the reindeer,' added Dad. 'They've flown a long way.'

Lulu and Rosie danced with excitement.

'Apples?' asked Rosie.

'Carrots,' said Lulu. 'I'm putting some carrots in my *klompen*.'

The three children ran to the kitchen.

Gus found a bunch of carrots in the fridge. Rosie fetched a glass of apple juice. Lulu carefully placed a piece of choc-chunk shortbread on a plate. She put a little bag of biscuits beside it for Santa to take home to Mrs Claus.

The children arranged the snacks on the wooden chest in front of the couch. Rosie ran outside to the garden. She brought back a frangipani flower and added it to the plate. Lulu and Gus put a carrot into each one of her clogs and placed it by the fireplace. Then they laid out their new letters to Santa.

Rosie looked warily at the fireplace.

'Dad, is Santa going to come down the chimney into our house?' asked Rosie.

Everyone looked at the fireplace.

'Straight down the chimney with a big sack of presents,' said Dad.

Rosie frowned. 'It's a bit scary to imagine someone coming into the house in the middle of the night,' she said.

Dad lifted Rosie up in the air and swung her around. He pointed to Asha and Jessie. The two dogs were lying right beside the fireplace, their heads flopped on their paws.

'Do you think those big, brave dogs would let anyone scary into our house?' asked Dad.

Asha woofed at the sound of her name. Jessie smiled her big doggy smile. Rosie shook her head.

'Of course not,' said Dad. 'The dogs only let really lovely people into the house, don't they?'

Rosie nodded and smiled. Dad put her down again.

Lulu wasn't scared but she was very curious.

'I'm going to wait up for Santa and say hello,' she said. 'I want to say thank you.'

Mum laughed. 'Santa won't come down if anyone's awake. He knows if you've been naughty or good. And he *knows* if you're pretending to sleep.'

Lulu looked at the chimney. It seemed a bit narrow for a person to climb down.

'How does Santa fit down the chimney with such a big tummy and a huge sack?' asked Lulu.

Gus nodded. 'My piggy might get stuck in the *chimbley*.'

Mum leaned down and kissed Lulu on the forehead. She looked into Lulu's eyes and smiled.

'It's magic, Lulu,' said Mum. 'Christmas magic.'

Mum tucked everyone into bed and kissed them goodnight. Lulu lay in the darkness for what seemed like hours. She was going to wait up for Santa no

matter what. It would be so exciting to see him. Lulu was sure Santa wouldn't be cross if she was awake. He seemed so cheerful and jolly.

Lulu's ears strained to listen for strange sounds. Reindeer landing on the roof. Or the noise of someone sliding down the chimney. But all she could hear was the low murmur of Mum and Dad talking in the kitchen.

She closed her eyes for just a second. But when she opened them it was light. It was Christmas morning.

The house was quiet and still. Lulu jumped out of bed. She raced to the doorway and peeked into the lounge room. The room looked very different.

The glass on the chest was empty. The letters were gone. There was nothing on the plate except golden crumbs. Chunks

of chewed-up carrot were scattered on the floor beside the red clogs.

The three sacks were no longer hanging on the mantelpiece. Instead they lay stuffed and overflowing on the floor beside the hearth. And under the Christmas tree was a pile of presents wrapped in green and turquoise paper. Lulu felt her heart jump into her mouth.

'Rosie, Gus,' she cried. 'Wake up.'

Her brother and sister straggled in, yawning. They stood in the doorway and stared.

Lulu looked at her brother and sister with shining eyes.

'Santa's been,' Rosie said.

'Yay,' cried Gus.

'And I think this is going to be the best Christmas ever,' said Lulu.

LULU'S CHRISTMAS CRAFT

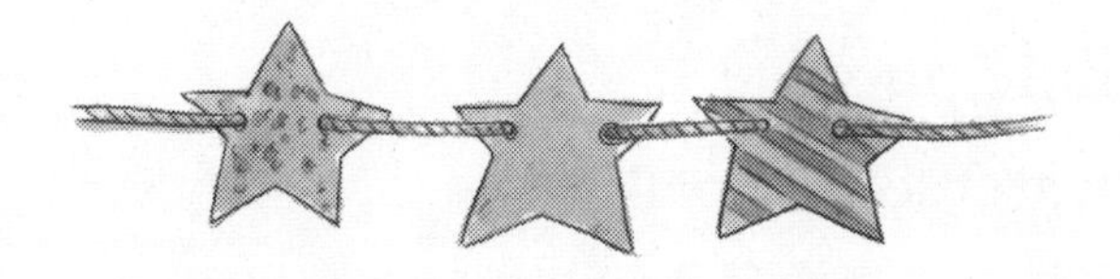

Make your own Christmas decorations and costumes with the help of Lulu and her artistic mum! Check with a parent or adult before you start any of these projects. They might be able to help you find the materials you need. And be sure to tell an adult before you use tricky tools such as scissors.

Paper Plate Decorations

These decorated Christmas shapes make lovely tree decorations or gift cards.

Materials

- paper plates
- pencil
- scissors
- hole puncher
- watercolour paint
- glue
- glitter, beads, silver stars, tinsel
- satin ribbon

Directions

- Draw an outline of an angel, butterfly, heart, bell or tree on each paper plate. The edge of the paper plate can create a pretty crinkled effect on part of the shapes, such as the angel wings and skirt.
- Use scissors to carefully cut out the shapes.
- With the hole puncher, make a hole in the top of each shape.
- Paint the shapes and then decorate them by gluing on beads, silver stars, glitter or tinsel.
- Allow the shapes to dry. Next, thread a piece of ribbon through the hole. Tie the ends of the ribbon together to make a loop for hanging your decoration.

Lulu and Rosie's Christmas Star Bunting

Materials

- cardboard
- scissors
- watercolour paint
- hole puncher
- jute string

Directions

- Draw a star on cardboard, and cut it out. Use it as a template to trace and cut out more stars.
- Paint the star shapes with watercolour paints. You could experiment with pale washes or streaky colouring.

Choose colours to match your Christmas colour scheme. While the paint is still wet, the stars can also be decorated with glitter, sparkles or letters that spell out 'Merry Christmas'.

- Allow the paint to dry. Then use the hole puncher to make two holes on opposite points of the star.
- Thread the stars onto your string and space them out evenly. The bunting can be hung above the front door, on the Christmas tree, across a window or on a wall.
- Painted stars can also be used as gift tags and cards, or individual decorations for the tree. Just put one hole in the top instead of two on the sides and add string.

Angel Costume

Materials

- white material or an old sheet
- scissors
- gold or silver tinsel
- cardboard
- stapler or glue
- glitter (optional)
- white ribbon or elastic
- ballet slippers (optional)

Directions

- Fold the material in half width-ways. When folded, the material needs to be long enough to cover the angel from shoulders to ankles. If the fabric is longer, carefully cut off the excess.

- Cut out a half circle at the fold to create a head hole. The sides can be sewn shut, or left open.
- Make a circlet from tinsel to fit around the angel's head. Knot the tinsel firmly and cut off any loose ends.

- Knot a length of tinsel around the child's waist to form a belt.
- Wings can be made by cutting two large wing shapes from cardboard and stapling or gluing them together. Decorate the wings with glitter or tinsel.
- To attach the wings, make two arm loops from white ribbon or elastic. Check that the angel can slip their arms through the loops before tying the loops off. Staple the loops to the wings.
- Angels can have bare feet or wear ballet slippers.

Easy Christmas Elf Costume

Materials

- green, red or stripy leggings or tights
- oversized green t-shirt (try getting a cheap one from an op shop)
- red Christmas elf hat (see the next activity)
- red scarf or strip of material
- gold bells to decorate (optional)

Note: If the weather is cool, the elf could wear a long-sleeved red or green t-shirt underneath.

Directions

- Cut a zigzag across the bottom of the oversized green t-shirt.
- You can also cut zigzags around the sleeves, or cut off the sleeves to create a tunic shape.
- Tie the red scarf or strip of material around the elf's waist to create a sash.
- Gold bells can be sewn on the end of the hat or on the hem of the tunic for decoration.
- Elves can wear riding boots, felt slippers, ballet slippers or bare feet.

Elf Hat

Materials

- A3 paper to make a template
- pencil
- red or green fabric (felt is good for a stiff hat, or you can cut up old t-shirts or leggings to make a floppier hat.)
- bells or buttons to decorate (optional)
- contrasting coloured felt or fake fur to trim around base (optional)

Method

- Draw a hat shape on paper (approximately 25 centimetres across the base and 30 centimetres high).
- Use the paper template to trace and cut out two identical shapes from your fabric.

- Sew the two fabric pieces together by hand or on the sewing machine.
- Turn the hat inside out so that the seams are hidden inside.
- Fold up the brim to form a cuff around the bottom.
- Decorate your elf hat by sewing a bell onto the top.
- You can also sew a contrasting fabric onto the base. The contrasting brim can be cut into a scalloped or zigzagged shape to make it more decorative.
- Extra buttons or bells could also be added to the brim to make it unique.

LULU'S FAVOURITE RECIPES

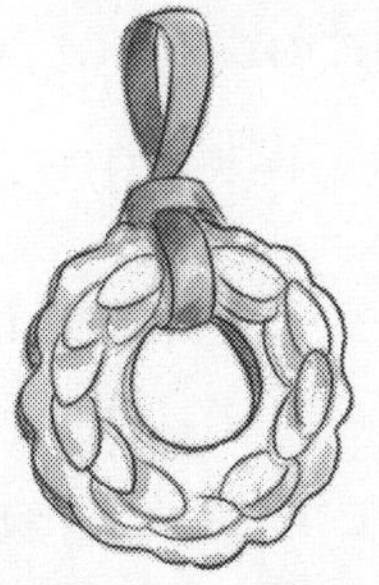

Lots of families have special recipes they make every Christmas. Here are the Bell family's favourite Christmas recipes.

Ask an adult to help you in the kitchen, and make cooking fun for the whole family, like Lulu, Rosie and Gus do.

Choc-Chunk Shortbread

Ingredients

- 125 grams butter
- ¼ cup brown sugar
- ½ cup white sugar
- 1 egg, beaten
- 1 ¼ cups plain flour
- ¼ teaspoon bicarbonate of soda (bicarb)
- 100–150 grams milk chocolate bits

Directions

- Preheat the oven to 180 degrees Celsius. Line two baking trays with baking paper.
- Cream the butter and brown and white sugars with an electric mixer.

- Add in the beaten egg and mix well.
- Stir in the flour and bicarb soda.
- Gently fold in the chocolate bits until they are evenly mixed through the dough.
- Wrap the dough in plastic cling wrap and store in the fridge overnight (or for up to three days).
- Teaspoon even amounts of cold dough onto baking trays. Press down lightly into rounded biscuit shapes. (Or you could use biscuit cutter shapes such as hearts or stars.)
- Cook for 10–15 minutes until light golden brown.
- Cool on a wire rack. When cool, place shortbread biscuits in cellophane bags and tie with ribbon.
- Shortbread can be stored in an airtight container for up to one week.

Kerstkransjes – Traditional Dutch Wreath Biscuits

These biscuits can be hung on the Christmas tree as edible decorations.

Ingredients

- grated zest of one lemon
- 160 grams butter
- ⅔ cup caster sugar
- 1 egg
- 2 ½ cups plain flour
- 1 teaspoon baking powder

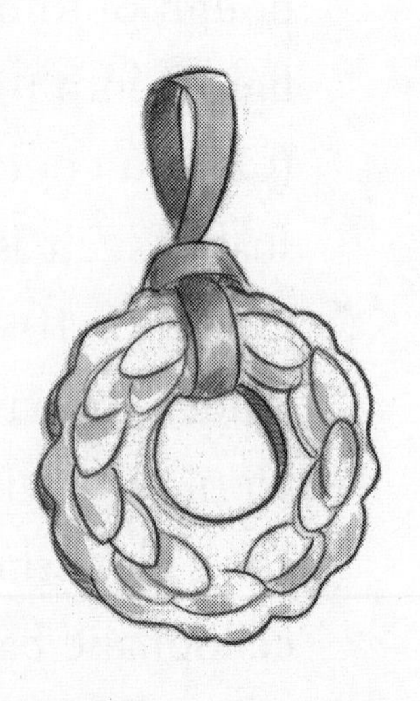

To decorate

- coloured ribbon
- 1 egg, beaten
- almond slivers, glacé cherries or melted chocolate

Directions

- Mix the lemon zest, butter, sugar and egg in a bowl.
- Add the baking powder and flour gradually.
- Knead the mixture into a dough. Wrap the dough with plastic cling wrap and place in the fridge for an hour or overnight.
- Preheat the oven to 180 degrees Celsius. Line two baking trays with baking paper.
- Take the chilled dough and knead again on top of the cling wrap.

* With a rolling pin, roll the dough out flat until it's about five millimetres thick.
* Use a round or star-shaped biscuit cutter to cut out the dough. Poke a small hole through the middle of each biscuit. Place biscuits on baking tray.
* Brush the biscuits with the beaten egg and decorate with almond slivers or glacé cherries. If you want to drizzle the biscuits with melted chocolate, bake them plain and decorate them when cool.
* Bake for 10–15 minutes until light golden brown.
* Cool on a wire rack. When cool, thread and tie coloured ribbon through the hole in each biscuit.

Lemon Butter as made by Lulu and her mum

Ingredients

- 1 cup lemon juice
- 2 cups white sugar
- 4 eggs, lightly beaten
- 250 grams butter (chopped into cubes to melt faster)

Directions

- Place ingredients in a small saucepan.
- Stir constantly over low heat until butter melts and ingredients mix. Keep stirring frequently for approximately 10 minutes or until mixture thickens.
- Pour into clean jars that have been sterilised in the dishwasher.

Lemon butter can be eaten on toast, muffins or scones. It can also be added to cakes or cupcakes. It keeps for about a month.

It is also great when cooked in a shortcake like this:

Shortcake base ingredients

- 125 grams butter
- 2 cups self-raising flour
- 1 cup caster sugar
- 2 eggs, lightly beaten

Shortcake base directions

- Preheat the oven to 160 degrees Celsius. Grease a cake or tart tin.
- In a medium-sized bowl, rub butter into flour and sugar. Mix until it resembles fine breadcrumbs.

- Make a well in the centre, and add eggs. Mix to form stiff dough.
- Press two-thirds of the mixture into the cake or tart tin.
- Pour hot lemon butter over the top, then crumble the remaining dough over the lemon filling.
- Bake for about 45 minutes or until golden.
- Cool in tin then dust with icing sugar before serving.

Chunky Home-Made Apple Sauce

Ingredients

- ½ lemon
- 6 Granny Smith apples
- ½ cup water
- 1 tablespoon brown sugar
- ground cinnamon and nutmeg

Directions

- Juice the lemon and finely zest the lemon skin.
- Peel and core the apples, then chop them into pieces.
- Place the apple pieces in a large saucepan with water and lemon juice.
- Bring to boil over medium heat.

- Allow to simmer, stirring frequently for 10–15 minutes until the apples are soft.
- Stir in sugar and lemon zest.
- Add a sprinkle of cinnamon and nutmeg. Additional sugar can be added if you prefer a sweeter sauce.

Apple sauce is perfect served hot with Christmas roast pork. It can also be served cold with leftovers.

Bell Family Saturday Breakfast Omelette

Ingredients

- 8 eggs
- 2 tablespoons milk
- 6 flat mushrooms
- red (Spanish) onion
- 250 grams feta cheese (or you could use grated cheddar or parmesan)
- approximately two teaspoons of fresh green herbs, e.g. chives, parsley, thyme or basil
- olive oil
- baby spinach leaves
- salt and pepper to taste

Directions

- Preheat grill.
- Whisk eggs in a bowl with a splash of milk until well mixed and frothy.
- Slice up mushrooms and red onion. Chop feta into cubes. Snip fresh herbs.
- Fry mushrooms and onion in a splash of olive oil for about five minutes until cooked.
- Add feta and baby spinach leaves. Pour egg mixture over the top of the mixture. Sprinkle fresh herbs on top.
- Allow to cook on the stovetop for 5–10 minutes, until the base is set but the top is still runny.

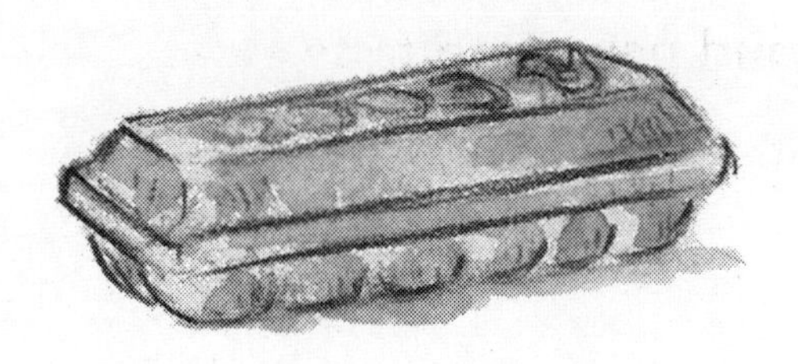

- Put the omelette pan under the hot grill to cook the top half for approximately 5 minutes, or until light golden brown.
- Serve on toast.

Note: You can also vary the recipe by adding chopped bacon, chopped tomato or sliced capsicum at the frying stage.

Dad's Famous Home-Made Burgers

Ingredients

Patties

- 1 kilogram beef or pork mince (or mixture of two)
- 1 onion, finely chopped
- 2 eggs, lightly whisked
- fresh basil, snipped
- 1 teaspoon Dijon mustard
- salt and pepper to taste

To serve

- hamburger buns, bread rolls or Turkish bread
- sliced tomato
- sliced cheese

- pineapple slices (optional)
- beetroot slices (optional)
- iceberg lettuce, shredded

Directions

- In a large bowl, place mince, onion, whisked eggs, basil and mustard. Season with salt and pepper.
- Mix ingredients together with clean hands.
- Shape mixture with your hands to create patties.
- Ask Mum or Dad to barbecue the patties until cooked. Top with a slice of cheese until slightly melted.
- Lightly warm or toast your bread.
- Serve meat patties on warm bread with your choice of salad. Lulu loves her burger with the works!

Read all the Lulu Bell books

Lulu Bell and the Birthday Unicorn

Lulu Bell and the Fairy Penguin

Lulu Bell and the Cubby Fort

Lulu Bell and the Moon Dragon

Lulu Bell and the Circus Pup

Lulu Bell and the Sea Turtle

Lulu Bell and the Tiger Cub

Lulu Bell and the Pyjama Party

Lulu Bell and the Christmas Elf

Plus more to come!

About the Author

Belinda Murrell grew up in a vet hospital and Lulu Bell is based on some of the adventures she shared with her own animals. After studying Literature at Macquarie University, Belinda worked as a travel journalist, editor and technical writer. A few years ago, she began to write stories for her own three children – Nick, Emily and Lachlan. Belinda's books include the Sun Sword fantasy trilogy and her children's novels *The Locket of Dreams*, *The Ruby Talisman*, *The Ivory Rose*, *The Forgotten Pearl*, *The River Charm* and *The Sequin Star*.

www.belindamurrell.com.au

About the Illustrator

Serena Geddes spent six years working with a fabulously mad group of talented artists at Walt Disney Studios in Sydney before embarking on the path of picture book illustration in 2009. She works both traditionally and digitally and has illustrated more than twenty books, ranging from picture books to board books to junior novels.

www.serenageddes.com.au

F[illegible]
NIGHTS
THROUGHOUT
THE
YEAR

Terry and Mimi Reilly
with
Jerry and Marilyn Burbach

1978
ABBEY PRESS, St. Meinrad, Indiana 47577

ISBN: 0-87029-136-x
Abbey Press
St. Meinrad, IN 47577
Designed & illustrated by Paul Grout

Library of Congress
Catalog Card Number: 77-92688

Dear Friends in Christ,

Welcome to this Family Night book! We hope you open it often to love, to share and to celebrate as a family. There are mini-chapters for each week of the year with oodles of ideas to enjoy. We wish you well and pray Family Night becomes a regular event in your family life as it is in ours.

Happy Family Nighting!

With affection, in Christ,

the Reilly
and
the Burbach
families

CONTENTS—Themes

INTRODUCTION

"What is" and "how to" *Family Night:*

1. *Family Night?*—It is time for families to be together, to pray, to study, to share and to play. Most often it involves the entire family at home.
2. How to?—Really it's simple. Someone in the family takes charge for the evening. The leader may use the outlines in this book. The outlines have ideas to plan some time together for faith and fun. The evenings follow the plan of OPENING PRAYER, ACTIVITY TIME, SNACK, ENTERTAINMENT, SHARING, CLOSING PRAYER.
3. Which night is best?—Any night during the week is good, although perhaps a Saturday morning or Sunday afternoon is best for you. Our family has found, by experience, that it is best to select one special time and then stick to it from then on. Monday night is our *Family Night* and our children look forward to it with great anti-

4. Do Mom and Dad have to be expert teachers?—No, *Family Night* is rather a time to be together, share ourselves and celebrate being a family.

WELCOME NEW YEARS

OPENING PRAYER

Dear Lord, thank you for this wondrous week with the birth of Christ, your only Son. Keep our hearts open to him as our Lord, Brother and Savior. Bless our family this evening and all your families everywhere. Open us to this coming New Year and fill it with your presence and love. *Amen.*

ACTIVITY TIME

Tonight, with the New Year almost here, it's time for us to take stock of ourselves as individuals and as a family. For most of us, there is thanksgiving in our hearts for this past year with the many jobs it has brought us. There were struggles too—maybe a job loss, a car wreck, someone ill, even a death of a friend or loved one. Now a New Year is beckoning, waiting to greet each of us, and it is full of surprises.

Choose one or more:

1. Inventory Time. Each of the family take a turn finishing the following for the rest to share:

a. the best thing about last summer . . .
b. the most joyful time on our family vacation . . .
c. the biggest crisis . . .
d. the most interesting person I met . . .
e. the hardest thing I had to do . . .
f. this New Year I would like our family to: be more . . . do more . . . go more to . . .

2. Read aloud Ecclesiastes 3:1-8 and 2 Timothy 1:9-13. Take next year's calendar and mark one day a month to be a family time for prayer and discussion of family needs.

3. Each make a list of four ways he has grown this year and then one way the family has grown. Share together.

SNACK

Salted nuts, pretzels and cold drinks.

ENTERTAINMENT

Charades. Take turns acting out famous movies or books.

SHARING

1. Share something each would like to see happen this coming New Year.

2. Share a special joy from the past couple of days.
3. Share a time when someone felt alone or left out.

CLOSING PRAYER

—Suggested Prayer: Dear Lord, thank you for this past year and all it meant to our family. Let us shine forth your love this coming year like a bright candle does in a darkened room. May your light shine in our hearts and may joy be written on our faces. Bless this coming year, Oh Lord, and bless us in your service. *Amen.*

12TH NIGHT'S GLITTER AND GLOW

OPENING PRAYER

We shout for joy, praise you, our God, with hearts filled with gladness! Emmanuel has come, our Savior, Christ the Lord. In this New Year help our family to sing your praises through words and deeds. Holy is your name, Lord Jesus, we adore you. *Amen.*

ACTIVITY TIME

This week of January 6th welcomes the feast of Epiphany or "Three Kings Day." It is also known as Twelfth Night and in many European countries, gifts are shared this night rather than at Christmas. As the season of Christmas draws to a close, the New Year ahead promises new horizons and adventures for each of us. Although it's time we put away all the season's decorations, the tinsel and lights, the candy canes, the tree, Christ is not put away. His presence is planted in our renewed hearts once again to grow and blossom and bear good fruit this New Year.

Choose one or more of the following:

1. The Potato Tree. *Materials:* toothpicks, one large potato, glass, water. Place the toothpicks about 1/3 down the side of the potato and place it in the glass. Fill the glass with water. Share some thoughts on how the potato will grow and change over the coming weeks. How can we grow with Christ planted in our hearts? Place the potato in a sunny location for the family to observe its growth.

2. Scripture. *Materials:* Bible. Read aloud 2 Tim 1:9,10 and also Galatians 5:13-26. Share some thoughts on areas the family can work on in this New Year to grow in the fruit of the Spirit.

3. Take down the Christmas tree and other decorations. Have each family member share his or her feelings about the season coming to a close. (You may wish to place the Christmas tree outside with bits of popcorn, bread crusts, strings of cranberries or salt for the birds to enjoy.)

4. Hold a family 12th Night party with everyone dressing up in costumes and exchanging small gifts.

SNACK

Anything goes—try a wild ice cream sundae experiment; but, what's created has got to be eaten.

ENTERTAINMENT

Play a favorite family game.

SHARING

1. Each share a moment he felt close to the newborn Christ Child.
2. Share a time someone felt shy and then what happened.
3. Share a happy moment from last week.

CLOSING PRAYER

—Suggested Prayer: Oh, Sweet Child Jesus, thank you for this beautiful evening. Help us to be open to your love in others this New Year and help us, also, to be instruments of your peace in a tension-filled world. Bless our family and your families everywhere, little Lord Jesus. *Amen.*

CELEBRATE KING WINTER

OPENING PRAYER

Dearest Father, as the chill of winter engulfs us outside, we thank you for our cozy home and the warmth it brings us. Bless our family this evening as we celebrate *Family Night*. Father, we remember those who are alone with no family; touch them with your love. *Amen*.

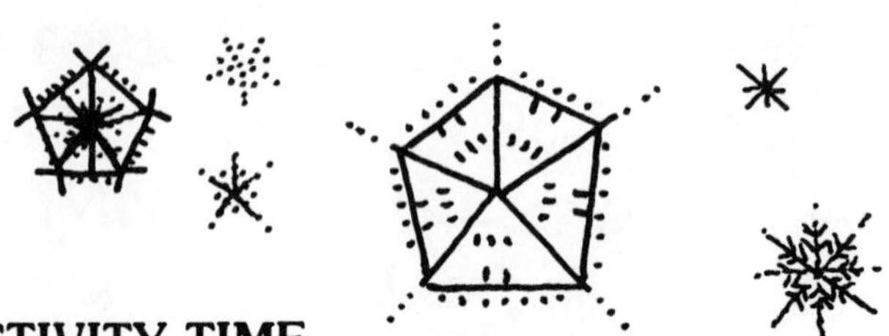

ACTIVITY TIME

Young Family

What makes winter? *Materials:* 2 balls, paper, pens, tape, string (optional: book showing rotation of earth around sun). Tape string around the center of one ball for the earth's equator. Have someone hold the other ball and be the sun. Explain and demonstrate how the earth circles the sun to create the seasons of the year. Take turns letting different children hold the earth ball and circle the sun ball. Then each write a paragraph or draw a picture entitled, "Thank you, Father, for King Winter."

Middle Years Family

Think winter. *Materials:* paper, pens, scissors, tape. For fun, take the word WINTER and each write as many words as possible using its letters W-I-N-T-E-R. Compare papers, see who got the most. Make a crown for King Winter and crown the winner. Then let each member of the family take a turn finishing the following for the rest to share:

a. Winter reveals God to me by . . .
b. Winter makes me feel . . .
c. Winter keeps me from . . . but lets me . . .
d. Winter teaches our family . . .

Adult Family

Scripture Time. *Materials:* Bible. Read aloud Genesis 8:22. In what way does winter seem like death? What can it tell us about our death and then after life?

SNACK

Hot cocoa or snow men ice cream sundaes (vanilla ice cream, raisins, nuts, cherries).

ENTERTAINMENT

Bundle up, take a short walk and make a list of signs of "King Winter."

SHARING

1. Share a moment someone felt frozen solid.
2. Each share what he likes the most about *Family Night.*
3. Someone share a time he felt especially loved.

CLOSING PRAYER

—Suggested Prayer: Wonderful Father, thank you for the seasons of the year and how they help to reveal your majesty to us. Bless our family this week and keep us ever open to witness kindness and love to all we meet. Thank you, Father, for *Family Night. Amen.*

MISSIONARY CALL

OPENING PRAYER

Dear Lord, hear our prayers this evening for our missionaries in our country and foreign lands. Strengthen them to promote your love by providing material and spiritual goods to their people. Strengthen their faith and their dedication. Bless our family tonight and keep us mindful of your missionary call. *Amen.*

ACTIVITY TIME

Start your *Family Night* at dinner tonight with a missionary meal of rice, a little baked fish, hot tea.

Young Family

Where Missionaries Work. *Materials:* large poster board, book with a world map, crayons. Discuss together where missionaries may be living. Copy the world map on the poster and color in all the areas in the world where the family thinks missionaries go. At the top mark "Missionary Call." Share thoughts on what kind of a person would become a missionary. Choose one missionary place in the world to pray for this week. Keep the poster in the eating area for the week.

Middle Years Family

Missionary Qualities. *Materials:* dictionary, paper, pens. Look up the word, "missionary" or "mission" in the dictionary. Share thoughts on what qualities a missionary needs. List seven on the paper. Do we need any of these qualities in our daily lives? Let each person answer the question: What would be the hardest thing for me if I were a missionary?

Adult Family

Scripture Time. *Materials:* Bible. Matthew 28:19 and then Mark 16:15. Has any family member known a missionary in person? What was most special about him? Are we each a missionary also? Share thoughts.

For All

1. Evaluate the family budget and see if a portion could be given to the missions, more than the family is currently giving.

2. Families interested in missionaries may wish to subscribe to the Maryknoll Magazine for $1.00 per year. Write to Maryknoll, N. Y. 10545.

SNACK AND ENTERTAINMENT

Banana Spree: Hold a race giving each family member a banana to peel and then eat. The winner is to be awarded a homemade button entitled: "Bananas—People and Monkeys Love 'em!"

SHARING

1. Each share one thing he likes about himself.
2. Each share one place he would go if he could go anywhere in the world for free.
3. Someone share a time he felt especially proud of his family.

CLOSING PRAYER

—Suggested Prayer: Dearest Jesus, thank you for this *Family Night.* Thank you, too, for the love in our family. Bless all your families everywhere, Jesus, but especially those who are ministered to by missionaries. *Amen.*

OUR FAMILY— PAST AND PRESENT

OPENING PRAYER

O Lord, how great is your love! The oceans are not large enough to hold it; the mountains not tall enough to reach it. Only our human hearts, small and fragile as they are can search inward through prayer and begin to discover the universe of your love. Thank you, dearest

God, for hearts, for prayer and for you. Our most wondrous God, be with us tonight. *Amen.*

SOMETHING TO THINK ABOUT

Who has reflected on the mystery of where our family begins and another one ends? It's a bit like which comes first, the chicken or the egg? We all "come from parents, grandparents and great-grandparents and, more than likely, will be all of them too. Past and present and future in our families are all linked together a bit like a big, huge bright colored circle. Where do we start and where do we end? Does the past hold the key to the future? Answers, anyone?

ACTIVITY TIME

Young Family

Family Tree. *Materials:* old family heirlooms, poster board, colored construction paper, crayons, glue, scissors. If possible, try to trace the family back to when some family member arrived in America from overseas. Create a Family Tree starting then. It can be any size. Be creative. Use different colors, shapes to denote generations and also separate colors for Mom's and Dad's relatives. Survey the family heirlooms and tell the story about their origin and why they are treasured.

Middle Years Family

Relatives—Where? *Materials:* book with a USA map, paper, crayons. Draw a good size map of the USA. Then note where relatives live. Write the foreign countries below if some live overseas or in Canada or Mexico. List five reasons why it's good to have relatives. Surprise a relative with a phone call.

Adult Family

Scripture Time. *Materials:* Bible. Read aloud Matthew 1:1-7. What is important about this passage? What does it say about our own backgrounds?

SNACK

Hot spiced tea and white cup cakes with coconut frosting (snowball delight).

ENTERTAINMENT

Future Telling. Write each family member's name on a piece of paper in secret and pass out the papers (no one is allowed to have his own name). Then each one write a long paragraph on what is going to happen to the person whose name he has drawn in the future. Be really creative. It's such fun! Read aloud and have the family guess who the person is.

SHARING

1. Each share one thing he's proud about in the family's history.
2. What was best about yesterday? Do share it.
3. Share a moment someone felt close to God.

CLOSING PRAYER

—Suggested Prayer: Lord, hear our prayer for our family members who have died. Lord, we also pray for those new members who have not even yet been born. Thank you tonight, Lord, and bless us as we strive to serve you daily. *Amen.*

For Lenten *Family Nights* begin on page 26

In 1978, Ash Wednesday is February 8 and Easter Sunday is March 26.

In 1979, Ash Wednesday is February 28 and Easter Sunday is April 15.

In 1980, Ash Wednesday is February 20 and Easter Sunday is April 6.

In 1981, Ash Wednesday is March 4 and Easter Sunday is April 19.

In 1982, Ash Wednesday is February 24 and Easter Sunday is April 11.

LOVE IS HELPFUL

I HELP-

1 ____
2 ____
3 ____
4 ____
5 ____
6 ____
7 ____
8 ____
9 ____
10 ____

I AM HELPED-

1 ____
2 ____
3 ____
4 ____
5 ____
6 ____
7 ____
8 ____
9 ____
10 ____

OPENING PRAYER

King of Glory, we praise you! We honor you! We worship you! How wondrous you are O Lord! Help us to taste your love in our family and to treasure one another as you treasure each of us. *Amen.*

SOMETHING TO THINK ABOUT

February, the month of love, bids us welcome. Loving in one's family is being willing to consider others and their needs as much as we consider our own. Jesus reminds us of this when he speaks in John

13:34. "I give you a new commandment: LOVE ONE ANOTHER. SUCH AS MY LOVE HAS BEEN FOR YOU, SO MUST YOUR LOVE BE FOR EACH OTHER. " Being helpful is one way to say "I love you." Tonight let's discover ways we are helpful and dream up even more. Love is proven through actions.

ACTIVITY TIME

Young Family

"I help . . . I am helped." *Materials:* plain, white sheets of paper, crayons, pens. Each family member should make a chart entitled "Ways I help at home." Go over the day from early morning to bedtime. Share ideas on ways each is helpful to others. Each list at least ten ways he is helpful. Turn the chart over and on the back side write

"Ways I am helped at home." Go through the day again and make a new list to go on the back. Do we really need one another? How? Keep the charts taped to the kitchen wall this week.

Middle Years Family

Family Help Function. *Materials:* Bible and ??? Read aloud 1 John 3:18. Share thoughts. Together plan a Family Help Function. Examples: welcome a new neighbor with a small gift; bring a cutting from a favorite plant to a convalescing friend. It could be a project around the house. Each share two thoughts about being helpful.

Adult Family

Scripture Time. *Materials:* Bible, paper, pens. Read aloud Philippians 2:1, 3-4. Recall from last week three instances when someone loved enough to offer to help. Write an informal thank you note to someone who helped the family in some way recently.

SNACK

Make a cherry treat, cobbler or pie.

ENTERTAINMENT

Play one of the games the family got for Christmas and has forgotten about.

SHARING

1. Each share what he likes best about belonging to the family.
2. Share an embarrassing moment from yesterday.
3. Share a time when someone felt especially grateful.

CLOSING PRAYER

—Suggested Prayer: Dear Jesus, remind us this week to be especially helpful to one another in our families and to others at school and at work. Thank you, Jesus, for love. *Amen.*

"VALENTINES"— LAVISH LOVE

OPENING PRAYER

O Gentle Lord, Father of life, Father of love, you are Father of all things, all places and all peoples. We praise you, gentle Father. Our hearts are filled with yearning to know you, to love you, to taste your presence among our families. Teach us, O Lord, to pray. *Amen.* (Say together the Lord's Prayer.)

SOMETHING TO THINK ABOUT

Valentine's Day is one special day during the year set aside in honor of LOVE. Love is the queen of all the virtues and is shared with us through the Scripture, John 3:16. "Yes, God so loved the world that he gave his only Son that whoever believes in him may not die, but may have eternal life." And to make the point even clearer, we are reminded in 1 John 4:11 "Beloved, if God has loved us so, we must have the same love for one another."

ACTIVITY TIME

Young Family

Valentines made with love. *Materials:* red and white construction paper, glue, scissors, bits of bright colored material, pens and crayons. Create homemade valentines with made up verses to send to favorite people. Also make some to mail to forgotten relatives, friends or the elderly in the community.

Middle Years Family

Valentine Surprises. *Materials:* shoe box, aluminum foil, red paper or ribbon, small pieces of paper, pens. Cover and decorate the shoe box making a slot in the top through which to insert small envelopes or slips of paper. Each person write down on the slips of paper a love message which includes a compliment and a good deed he plans to do for each family member before Valentine's Day. Keep a copy as a reminder and place one in the box to be shared on February 14th. Use the box as a dinner table centerpiece all during the week.

Adult Family

Love Notes. *Materials:* Bible, small index cards, pens. Make place card "love notes," one for each day until Valentine's Day. Place each person's name on the front and write something loveable about that person. Use at the dinner table to mark the places of family members at mealtime. Read aloud 1 John 4:19-21. Share thoughts on how it relates to the family.

SNACK

Strawberry sodas and valentine-shaped cookies.

ENTERTAINMENT

Giggle Engine. Gather together in a line. One person is the engine operator and can turn it on or off, high speed or low speed. See how well everyone can obey the orders. The one who can't stop giggling becomes the engine operator. Try to catch everyone.

SHARING

1. Each share: Love means to me . . .
2. Each share what is most fun for him about Valentine's Day.
3. Share a favorite memory from a Valentine's Day in the past.

CLOSING PRAYER

—Suggested Prayer: Gentle Lord, thank you for the love we sensed in our family tonight. Thank you for loving all of us, your children. We praise you, O wonderous God. *Amen.*

LOVE IS OBEDIENT

OPENING PRAYER

God is Love

Gentle Lord, King of Glory,
Gentle Lord, King above,
Gentle Lord, fill our spirits
With the mysteries
of your love.

Amen

SOMETHING TO THINK ABOUT

In the Scriptures, Christ gives us two commands to be obeyed. Matthew 22:36-40, "Love the Lord your God with all your heart, soul and mind. This is the first and most important commandment. The second most important is similar: Love your neighbor as yourself." As we grow in love for one another and place others' needs before our own, obedience loses its sting and can become a source of great joy in the family and larger community. Tonight let's look at obedience. All read together Ephesians 6:1-4.

ACTIVITY TIME

Young Family

Love Banner. *Materials:* felt or burlap, rod and string, scissors, glue. Together create a banner. Examples, "Love Makes Obedience Easier" or "Moms, Dads and kids work at obedience." Mom and Dad share some areas each is working in at being obedient. For example, work or traffic laws. Discuss some family rules and the "why" behind them.

Middle Years Family

Rules are important. *Materials:* large poster board, felt tip pens. Together make up a list of rules that the family observes. Hold a discussion on them. Are there any that may need to be changed, updated or done away with? Should any new ones be added? Share thoughts about how rules are meant to guide us in our life of love. How do rules in the family help us to show our love for one another? Write the rules on the poster and place it in a common family area.

Adult Family

Scripture Time. *Materials:* Bible, dictionary. Read aloud Ephesians 6: 1-4. Then look up key words in the dictionary. Share thoughts on how the passage may be applied in the family more effectively.

SNACK

Cranberry punch and cookies.

ENTERTAINMENT

Plan a family Mardi Gras celebration for the Tuesday before Ash Wednesday. Horns, costumes, skits, even a special dinner that night might be in order. Have a family member do some research and share about the history and purpose of Mardi Gras.

SHARING

1. Share a time someone found it very hard to be obedient.
2. Share a moment when each wished he lived elsewhere.
3. Share a favorite family moment from the past week.

CLOSING PRAYER

—Suggested Prayer: Dear Lord, thank you for love. We know love is the gift you give all of us and the gift you want us to share with others, especially all the members of our family. Help us to love each other as you loved us. *Amen.*

1st WEEK OF LENT

Theme: Temptation, Repentance

OPENING PRAYER

Most Heavenly Father, tonight we gather in your name for our first lenten *Family Night*. Be with us this evening, dear Lord, and help us prepare our hearts through sacrifice, penance and good works during these forty days of Lent. We pray for your families throughout our nation and we especially remember your families who are suffering and in pain. Bless this evening, O Lord, and each of us present. *Amen.*

LESSON: Use one of the following formats

Young Family

Materials: flower pot, dirt, 3 flower bulbs, or seeds, old newspapers. Planting bulbs, or seeds, to bloom for Easter is so exciting for small children. Watching them grow from week to week is a golden opportunity for us to compare the bulbs or seeds to us and our lives. As we respond in love to God's light we grow. We are watered by study and sharing and continue to grow. The bulbs or seeds can be passed around and studied and be compared to our sinfulness; but as they grow, as we do through water and light, they look very different from their original form. The family can share about ways each can grow in Lent through good deeds and little sacrifices each can make for God. If desired, a list may be made of ideas. (Next week: find one large jar or can with cover.)

Middle Years Family

Materials: Bible. One member of the family read Romans: chapter 5, verse 12, verses 17-19. Describe what differences there are in thoughts, feelings and actions between saying "I'm sorry" and being sorry from our hearts. Each might share one example of both of the above moments from his own experience. Read Mt 4:1-11 (Jesus' temptation).

—Name some ways we can each be tempted.

—Share some ideas on what to do when we feel we're being tempted.

Adult Family

Materials: Bible. Read aloud Gn 2:7-9 and 3:1-7 (pause, each share thoughts) next, Romans 5:12-19 (again, a sharing of thoughts) and then Mt 4:1-11. Each person may share a moment from the past when he or she was really deeply sorry for some deed and describe what that moment was like and then what did he or she do to make amends.

SNACK: Take turns having a different family member in charge each week.

ENTERTAINMENT: Favorite family game or activity the whole family can enjoy.

SHARING

This can be a very special time for the family. It's a time to listen closely to one another and experience some empathy. Encourage one another especially to share his feelings. The whole family can taste precious moments of intimacy and unity together during this sharing time.

CLOSING PRAYER

—Group spontaneous prayer.

—Scripture.

—Lord's Prayer and Hail Mary.

—Suggested prayer—Dearest Father, thank you for allowing us to share together in our *Family Night*. Forgive us for our many offenses and help us to really grow as a loving family this season of Lent. Bless each of us and allow us to carry your spirit of renewal within and to spread reconciliation through love to all we meet this coming week. We love you, Father. *Amen*.

APPENDIX

Optional daily scriptural readings

The following scriptures are provided for families who wish to have a daily devotional time during Lent in addition to their *Family Night*. The scripture may be read and sharing reactions and opinions regarding the passage is encouraged. The devotional can begin and end with prayer.

Week I

Sunday	Genesis 2:7-9, 3:1-7; Romans 5:12-19; Mt 4:1-11
Monday	Leviticus 9:1, 2, 11-18; Mt 25:31-46
Tuesday	Isaiah 55:10, 11; Mt 6:7-15
Wednesday	Jonah 3:1-10; Luke 11:29-32
Thursday	Esther 4:12-16, 23-25; Mt 7:7-12
Friday	Ezekiel 18:21-28; Mt 5:20-26
Saturday	Dt 26:16-19; Mt 5:43-48

Week II

Sunday	Genesis 12:1-14; 2 Timothy 1:8-10; Mt 17:1-9
Monday	Daniel 9:4-10; Luke 6:36-38
Tuesday	Isaiah 1:10, 16-20; Mt 23:1-12
Wednesday	Jeremiah 18:18-20; Mt 20:17-28
Thursday	Jeremiah 17:5-10; Luke 16:19-31
Friday	Genesis 37:3, 4, 12, 13, 17-28; Mt 21:33-46
Saturday	Micah 7:14, 15, 18-20; Luke 15:1-3, 11-32

Week III

Sunday	Exodus 17:3-7; Romans 5:1, 2, 5-8; John 4:5-42
Monday	2 Kings 5:1-15; Luke 4:24-30
Tuesday	Daniel 3:25, 34-43; Mt 18:21-35
Wednesday	Dt 4:1, 5-9; Mt 5:17-19
Thursday	Jeremiah 7:23-28; Luke 11:14-23

Friday	Hosea 14:2-10; Mark 12:28-34
Saturday	Hosea 6:1-6; Luke 18:9-14

Week IV

Sunday	1 Samuel 16:1, 6, 7, 10-13; Ephesians 5:8-14; John 9:1-41
Monday	Isaiah 65:17-21; John 4:43-54
Tuesday	Ezekiel 47:1-9, 12; John 5:1-3, 5-16
Wednesday	Isaiah 49:8-15; John 5:17-30
Thursday	Exodus 32:7-14; John 5:31-47
Friday	Wisdom 2:1, 12-22; John 7:1, 2, 10, 25-30
Saturday	Jeremiah 11:18-20; John 7:40-53

Week V

Sunday	Ezekiel 37:12-14; Romans 8:8-11; John 11:1-45
Monday	Daniel 13:41-62; John 8:1-11
Tuesday	Numbers 21:4-9; John 8:21-30
Wednesday	Daniel 3:14-20, 91, 92, 95; John 8:31-42
Thursday	Genesis 17:3-9; John 8:51-59
Friday	Jeremiah 20:10-13; John 10:31-42
Saturday	Ezekiel 37:21-28; John 11:45-57

Holy Week

Passion Sunday	Isaiah 50:4-7; Phil 2:6-11; Mt 26:14-27, 66
Monday	Isaiah 42:1-7; John 12:1-11
Tuesday	Isaiah 49:1-6; John 13:21-33, 36-38
Wednesday	Isaiah 50:4-9; Mt 26:14-25
Holy Thursday	Exodus 12:1-8, 11-14; 1 Cor 11:23-26; John 13:1-15
Good Friday	Isaiah 52:13-15, 53:1-12, Hebrews 4:14-16, 5:7-9; John 18:1-19, 42
Holy Saturday	Genesis 1:1-31, 2:1, 2; Romans 6:3-11; Mt 28:1-10

Easter Sunday Acts 10:34, 37-43; Col 3:1-4; John 20:1-9

2nd WEEK OF LENT

Theme: Vision & Renewal

OPENING PRAYER

Our family gathers tonight in your presence to share with one another in love. Lord, thank you for this evening and the opportunity for us to come together for *Family Night*. We pray for the presence of your Holy Spirit and for those we know who are lonely and also for those who have no one to love them. Help our family to reach out to such people. *Amen.*

LESSON

Young Family

Materials: 1 large jar or can with cover, glue, old magazines, scissors, plain paper. Make a lenten prayer jar. Have the children reflect on ways God can speak to them. (Example: through parents, friends, nature.) Everyone can cut out pictures that reflect his feelings and thoughts about conversation. The pictures may be arranged and glued to the jar. Each person can make three or four prayers about someone or something other than himself. Mom or Dad can help with the writing if necessary. The prayers may be placed in the jar to be used at closing prayer time in future *Family Nights*.

Middle Years Family

Materials: Bible, paper, pens. Read Scripture aloud, 2 Timothy 1:8-10 (pause in silence).

Renewal is what takes place within us and is ever so personal between each of us and our God. Reconciliation flows from a renewed spirit just like sun rays come from the sun itself. Reconciliation flows out upon everyone we meet through our senses of touch, of speech, the way we listen, the very look in our eyes.

Activities: Each person writes a letter to the family in answer to the questions (1) Who am I? and (2) How can I reveal myself to my family through ways of reconciliation? Take about 10 or 15 minutes to write and then the letters may be read aloud or exchanged and read silently as a family.

Adult Family

Materials: Bible. Read aloud Genesis 12:1-4 then 2 Timothy 1:8-10 and then Matthew 17:1-9.

Before we can really be serious about taking up our cross and following Christ we need to first experience him in some form of personal experience. The readings above show very boldly Abraham's and the apostles' "visions" and each had a long hard journey to follow after the experience. If anyone has had some experience of Christ in his life that made a strong impression, it would be worthwhile to share it this evening.

SNACK

ENTERTAINMENT (optional)

SHARING

—Each shares a high point during the week.

—Someone may share a low point or a struggle the past week.

—Each may share a moment he felt especially close to God.

CLOSING PRAYER

—Spontaneous: use prayer jar.

—Scripture: 2 Cor 5:17-19.

—Lord's Prayer and Hail Mary.

—Suggested prayer: Dearest Lord, thank you for this evening and for each member of our family. Help us to grow into a deeper awareness of one another's needs and help us to reach out to one another in love and healing. Help us to carry one another's burdens. We love you Lord, God and surrender our family wholly to you. Oh Lord, use our family to help build up your kingdom here on earth. *Amen.*

3rd WEEK OF LENT

Theme: Water

OPENING PRAYER

Dearest Lord Jesus, thank you for this past week and for the moments of love our family felt through your Holy Spirit who is ever present in our lives. We ask your blessing upon our *Family Night* as we gather in your name. We pray for our Bishop, priests, sisters and all God's people especially those in our diocese. Bless us during this year. *Amen.*

LESSON

Young Family

Materials: Bible, magazines, 1 large piece of paper, glue and scissors. The theme of Lent this week is water and how we grow. Check the flower pot from two weeks ago and share together what changes have taken place since the bulbs or seeds were planted. Water it and each can share ways water brings life. Make a large collage using a stiff paper or cardboard, old magazines or newspapers with "WATER" as the center and all that can happen from its presence coming out in all directions to fill the paper. Then read from the Bible John 4:13, 14. Just as we see what water can do for the earth, we know Jesus can do the same for our souls. Have the children reflect on what water means to them in our faith.

Middle Years Family

Materials: Bible, burlap, felt, glue, scissors. Water is this week's theme as we draw closer to Holy Week. Read John 4:5-26. Each may share what it meant to him. What are some ways our family as a whole can be living water for each other? What are some ways we, as a family, can share each other's burdens?

Activity: Make a banner together with *Family* and *Lent* as its theme. Hang in the eating area when finished. (Before starting be sure to plan out the banner on a piece of paper.)

Adult Family

Materials: Bible. Read aloud: Exodus 17:3-7, share Romans 5:1, 2 and 5-8, share thoughts John 4:5-26. Was there a time anyone was away from the Church for a while or felt remote from God? (Try to describe what it was like.) What was the returning experience like?

Activity: Is there anyone whom you know that is away from the Church or is feeling remote from our Lord? What can you do to help that person?

SNACK

ENTERTAINMENT (optional)

SHARING

A high point during the past week, a low point, a time each felt close to God.

CLOSING PRAYER

—Spontaneous: use prayer jar for the little ones.

—Scripture: John 4:14.

—Suggested prayer: Dear Lord, thank you for this evening and bless us in all we do this coming week. *Amen.*

4th WEEK OF LENT

Theme: Light

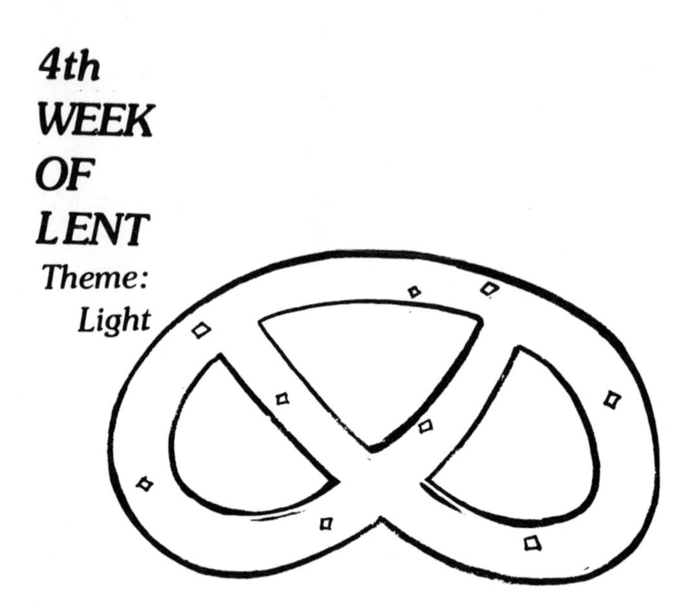

OPENING PRAYER

Dearest Lord, keep us faithful to our lenten sacrifices and help each of us to grow in holiness as Easter approaches. Bless our *Family Night* this evening and help us to be loving and open to one another. *Amen.*

LESSON

Young Family and Middle Years Family

The *Pretzel Story:* the pretzel has a deep spiritual meaning for Lent. It has been used in Lent for over 1500 years. The pretzel is made in the shape of the crossed arms, for in those days the people crossed their arms over their breasts while praying. The breads were called "little arms." Later the Germanic people coined the term "pretzel" which we use today. Bake:

SOFT PRETZELS

1 cake yeast dissolved into 1 1/2 cups warm water.
Add 1 teaspoon salt, and 1 tablespoon sugar.
Blend in 4 cups of flour.

Knead dough until smooth. Cut into small pieces. Roll into ropes, and twist into desired shape. Place on lightly greased cookie sheets. Brush pretzel with 1 beaten egg. Sprinkle with coarse salt. Bake immediately at 425° for 12 to 15 minutes. (For hard pretzels, use only 1 1/4 cups water and add 1/4 cup melted butter. Make pretzels smaller and bake until brown. These keep well over a period of days.)

PRETZEL PRAYER: We beg you, O Lord, to bless these breads which are to remind us that Lent is a sacred season of penance and prayer. For this very reason, the early Christians started the custom of making these breads in the form of arms crossed in prayer. Thus they kept the holy purpose of Lent alive in their hearts from day to day, and increased in their souls the love of Christ, even unto death, if necessary. Grant us, we pray, that we, too, may be reminded by the sight of these pretzels to observe the holy season of Lent with true devotion and great spiritual fruit. We ask this through Christ our Lord. *Amen.* (Taken from: *Pretzels for God*, St. Francis Xavier Church, Phoenix, Arizona.)

Adult Family

Materials: Bible, paper, pen. Read aloud Ephesians 5:8-14, pause, share thoughts and feelings; read John 9:1-41 or the shortened version John 9:1, 6-9, 13-17, 34-38. Together make up a list of ways the family lives in the light. Make another list of new ways our family can live more fully in God's "light." Paste on refrigerator for the coming week.

SNACK

ENTERTAINMENT (optional)

SHARING

Each shares a struggle he had during the past week, each shares a high point and a moment he felt especially close to some particular person in the family.

CLOSING PRAYER

—Spontaneous: use prayer jar.

—Scripture: John 8:12.

—Lord's Prayer and Hail Mary.

—Suggested prayer: Most Holy Father, we thank you for this evening and for our being gathered in prayer as a family. Bless us this coming week as we continue our lenten sacrifices in preparation for Easter. We love you, Father. *Amen.*

5th WEEK OF LENT

Theme: Atonement, Forgiveness

OPENING PRAYER

Dear Holy Spirit, tonight we come together to share and suffer in the process of bringing peace to our family and our community. Give us the power to be open and aware of your presence with us. Let us enter into this night and the remainder of Lent and this year with a forgiving attitude.

LESSON

Young Family

Play or skit. Have the family act out a family scene and all members switch roles. One of the kids could be Mom and another could be Dad. Likewise, the parents would act out the kids. Then have each member become angry at another member of the family. The parents could begin, pretending to be little brother and sister by fighting with one another or talking unkindly to a parent. This part would last for a very short time only. Next, each person should maintain the roles they have and ask forgiveness for being unkind to the other. This skit should be lighthearted and fun. After the skit, the parent(s) may ask each member to seek forgiveness from the other and exchange a sign of peace. The older children and adults should go through the lesson for *Middle Years* and *Adult Families.*

Middle Years Family and Adult Family

Read aloud Mt 5:23, 24. What does Jesus mean when he refers to "your gift"? Are these words of Jesus still applicable today? Why? Then each family member may give an example from his own experience that would fit the above Scripture reading.

Activity: Make peace with one or several family members by apologizing or asking forgiveness for a specific offense. This could be accomplished verbally or in writing. Forgive and forget—as our Lord forgives—no strings attached. All family members then exchange a sign of peace (an embrace is encouraged if the family is accustomed to it). Next, each family member selects a business acquaintance, past friend, neighbor or classmate with whom he is not at peace. During the next week he would seek out that person and reconcile himself. This often is a difficult and humbling experience. The experience may be shared during the next *Family Night*.

SNACK TIME

ENTERTAINMENT (optional)

SHARING

Either the usual weekly sharings or perhaps a more immediate feeling, hope or struggle, prompted by this evening's lesson.

CLOSING PRAYER

—Read aloud Mt 6:14, 15 and Mark 11:24, 25.

—Spontaneous prayer (use prayer jar).

—Lord's Prayer and Hail Mary.

—Suggested prayer: Dear Lord Jesus, thank you for suffering for us, for dying for our sins, for showing us the way to eternal life with you. Give us the strength this week to really understand forgiveness and to practice forgiveness with our brothers. *Amen.*

HOLY WEEK

Theme: Christ's Suffering

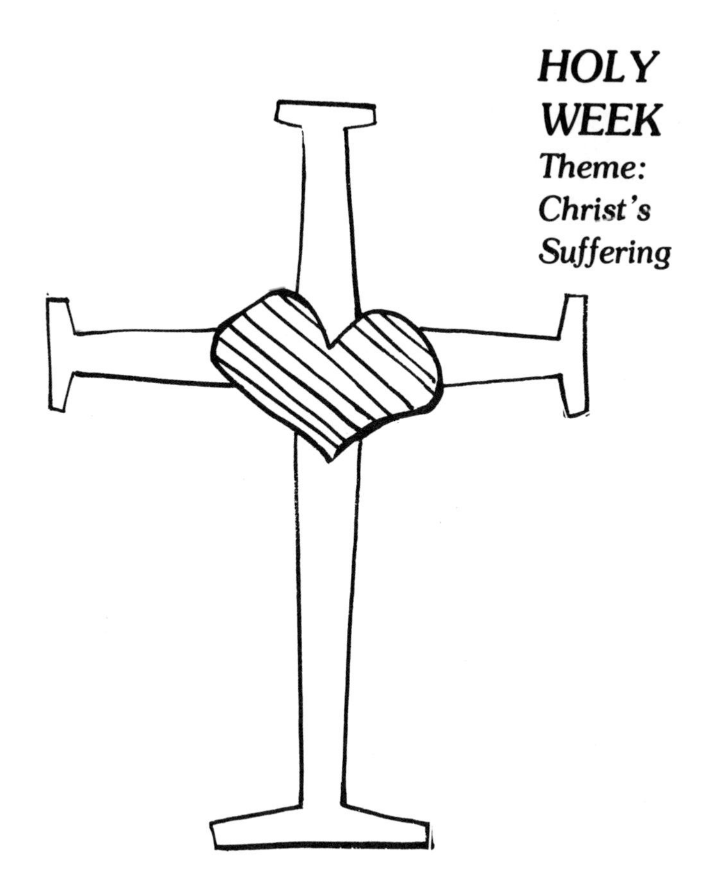

OPENING PRAYER

Dearest Jesus, tonight we gather once again in your name for our *Family Night*. Bless us this evening as we dwell upon this coming Holy Week and all you have suffered for each one of us. Help us to enter into the spirit of this entire week beginning with our family this evening. Thank you, dearest Jesus, for giving your life for all men so that we might dwell with you eternally. *Amen.*

LESSON

Young Family

Materials: Large piece of cardboard, old newspapers, scissors, blue, red crayon.

Activity: Cardboard cross. Cut cardboard into a large cross, together look through the newspapers to find pictures of suffering, or of violence. Cover the entire cross with the pictures just previously cut out. The completed cross may be hung in the family dining area all during Holy Week. Ask each member of the family to remember a time when he really suffered physical or mental pain and have him try to relive that moment, sharing it with the rest of the family. Each of us has suffered in some way. It might only be a scraped knee or it may be as serious as a death or critical illness. Have each share and then have him draw a red heart somewhere upon the cross to add his own suffering to that of our Lord's.

Middle Years Family and Adult Family

Materials: Bible. Read aloud Mt 27:11-54. After a few moments, each may share with the others what the Scripture meant to him personally this evening and also a moment from the past when he experienced tremendous suffering, physically or mentally. He also may share what it was like to see someone he loved suffer deep pain. How are our own sufferings united to the crucified Christ?

SNACK (optional)

Fasting is suggested.

ENTERTAINMENT

This time should also be altered to reflect Christ's Passion. This would be an ideal time for the family to plan their activities for Holy Week. Families are encouraged to actively participate in the observances that parishes provide. These unique community experiences at the parish level should prove to be an enriching experience for the whole family. The sacrament of reconciliation can provide members of the family with a uniquely meaningful insight during this time.

SHARING

—Share the experience of making peace with someone with whom you were not at peace (see lesson for last week).

—Some may share when they felt especially close to God during the past week.

—Share struggles and joys.

CLOSING PRAYER

—Spontaneous: (prayer jar).

—Scripture: Phil 2:8, 9

—Lord's Prayer.

—Suggested prayer: Most Holy Jesus, thank you for this evening and our family's sharings. Tonight we tasted but a small portion of your suffering for us. O, Lord Jesus, thank you for giving your life so that we might have life eternally with you. Help our family to make this Holy Week more meaningful through prayer, fasting, and our attendance at our parish Holy Week services. We praise you now and forever. *Amen.*

EASTER CELEBRATION

Theme: Alleluia & Baptism

OPENING PRAYER

"Holy, holy, holy Lord, God of power and might, heaven and earth are full of your glory." Our hearts are rejoicing, filled to overflowing with praise for you, Father, Son and Holy Spirit. Hear our family's praises along with all the thronging crowds of heaven. Jesus Christ is risen, Alleluia, Alleluia! Our family's hearts shout for joy. Alleluia. *Amen.*

LESSON

Easter is the time for renewal of baptismal promises, so tonight let us celebrate with a baptism party.

Young Family

Theme for the evening is white. (See *Snack* for advance preparations.) *Materials:* 1 tall white candle (cost 25c), 1 sprig of greens or flower for each member of the family, an empty jar or vase to hold the greenery, old pictures of each one's baptism (if available) or a special remembrance of that day.

Activity: The baptismal pictures may be shared for all to see and together try to relive the different historical moments of each family member's baptism. Next, form a procession with each one holding his sprig of greens or flower to symbolize his new life in Christ. Then light the white candle which is to be held by the father or household head. The room may be darkened to better show up the light of the candle, the symbol for the risen Christ in our midst. While proceeding single file to the prepared party table, sing together, ALL THE EARTH PROCLAIM:

All the earth proclaim the Lord. Sing your praise to God.

1. Serve you the Lord, heart filled with gladness,
   Come into his presence singing for joy.
4. Enter his gates bringing thanksgiving,
   O enter his courts while singing his praise.
6. Honor and praise be to the Father, the Son and the Spirit world without end.

Lent is over, Easter was yesterday, this truly is a time for rejoicing! "Celebrate."

Middle Years Family

Materials: 1 white candle, Bible. (See *Snack* for preparations.) Begin with lighting the candle, "Christ's presence with us" and singing ALL THE EARTH PROCLAIM (see above). Read aloud, Mt 28:1-10. What a moment it was for those women! There is no attempt to describe the Resurrection in any of the Gospels for there were no eyewitnesses. We are called for a response of faith and a commitment, therefore, to all that Christ spoke and to the example of his life; yesterday we did respond in faith, through the renewal of our baptismal promises. Together try to recall what was said yesterday and share feelings and ideas about the different promises and also the profession of faith. "Celebrate."

Adult Family

Materials: Bible, 1 white candle. The white candle may be lit to remind us of Christ's presence among us and of our calling to live in his new life. Read aloud, Acts 10:34, 37-43, then Col 3:1-4, share thoughts and feelings, then go on to read Mt 28:1-10. Together join in song ALL THE EARTH PROCLAIM, found above. "Celebrate."

SNACK

Baptismal Party. Prepare the table with a white tablecloth (or sheet) and white napkins; plan to serve a white cake and/or vanilla ice cream. The "candle" may be placed in the center of the table during the snack time along with the greens or flowers. The flower pot planted back on Feb. 17 may be used as part of the table centerpiece. Enjoy the party!

ENTERTAINMENT

If there are baptismal movies or slides, now would be a great time to watch them.

SHARING

—What does *Family Night* mean to our family?

—Share a high and low point of the week.

—Share when each felt most close to God during the week.

CLOSING PRAYER

—Spontaneous.

—Scripture: Phil 2:8, 9.

—Lord's Prayer and Hail Mary.

—Suggested prayer: Dearest Lord, thank you for this precious gift of new life through our Savior, Jesus Christ. Thank you, too, for this evening and what it has meant to our family. Praise you, now and forever. *Amen.*

VALUES MAKE US SPECIAL

OPENING PRAYER

Dearest Father, thank you for this past week and for all you have given our family. Thank you for our mountains, for our deserts in bloom, our brilliant colored sunsets and for all our friends and neighbors in this diocese. Bless each of us this evening and help us to respond more and more each day to your call to be ever open and filled with love, especially within our family. *Amen.*

LESSON

Each family has a specialness all its own that makes it the family others see. Often the family isn't aware of what makes its own specialness and importance. Every family member is very special and precious, too. He helps to make up the family's uniqueness, what makes it different from every other family. To help discover what each family's specialness is, let us share thoughts.

Young Family

Materials: Paper, crayons. Each divides his paper into four sections; a different picture is to be drawn in each block.

1. A picture of myself, showing my feelings about myself through color choice, example: yellow, sunny; blue, gentle, peaceful; orange, strong.
2. Draw the house or apartment the family lives in and decorate it with things that make it special to me.
3. Draw a picture of all the family members with colors showing my feelings about each person.
4. Draw a picture of the very best thing I like about my family.

After all have finished the drawings, each may have a chance to explain his picture, then name what he thinks is the most special thing about his family.

Middle Years Family

Materials: Paper, pencils, enough for each person. Pass out paper and pencils. The paper may be divided into three columns.

1. Make a list of five qualities I like most about myself; (this isn't as easy as it may seem; often we tend to be negative about ourselves).
2. Make a list naming all the members of the family and after each name list the three qualities I like most about that person.
3. In four sentences or less, name the family's most endearing quality and why I chose that particular quality.

Share and discuss what each has written.

Adult Family

Materials: Paper, pencils. Divide paper into three columns.

1. What am I most thankful for in my family? Why?
2. Name two qualities I most admire in each person of the family.
3. As a whole, what is my family's number 1 quality and how does it relate to God's presence in our family?

Share and discuss what each has written.

SNACK

ENTERTAINMENT

SHARING

—Each may share a high and low point of the last week.
—Each may share a moment he felt especially close to God.

CLOSING PRAYER

—Spontaneous prayer.
—Scripture: Ephesians 1:3-6.
—Lord's Prayer and Hail Mary.
—Suggested prayer: Dear Father, our family thanks you for this evening and for the qualities you have helped reveal to each of us. Thank you for loving us so much. Bless your Church and our Christian family throughout the world. Help each of us to build your kingdom on earth as we witness you wherever we are and whatever we do this coming week. *Amen.*

FRIENDS ARE TREASURES

OPENING PRAYER

Friends are treasures, Lord, and we thank you for all of them. A friend, Lord, helps reveal your goodness and beauty to us. Bless all our friends, dear God, and fill them with your love. Help us to be loving and faithful friends in return. *Amen.*

ACTIVITY TIME

Young Family

My Best Friends. *Materials:* paper plates, crayons, tape. Each person think of one person (not in the family) who was or is his very best friend ever. Each share who he chose and why. Then share the most fun time each shared with his friend. Each person, using about four paper plates, create a likeness of his best friend—hair, eyes, clothes, shoes. After all have finished, hang them in the eating area with a sign above them, "Thank you, God, for our good friends."

Middle Years Family

Qualities. *Materials:* paper, tape, aluminum foil, crayons, small boxes or blocks. Brainstorm together on what qualities make a friendship a great one. Narrow the list to around six to ten key qualities (example: mutual respect, faithfulness). Cover the boxes or blocks with foil and tape on pieces of paper marking a quality. Build the blocks into a pyramid with the most important quality at the top. Use the creation for a centerpiece at dinner this week. Each family member write a short paragraph to share with the family on why friends are important.

Adult Family

Scripture Time. *Materials:* Bible. Proverbs 18:24, Proverbs 22:24-25 and John 15:12-17. Share thoughts.

SNACK

Brownies and milk.

ENTERTAINMENT

See how many words the family can come up with that start with the letters in the word, "friendship," or call long distance a family friend who is out of town.

SHARING

1. Mom and Dad share about their favorite childhood friend. Tell a funny story about an adventure each shared with his or her friend.
2. Each share a high or low point from the past week.

CLOSING PRAYER

—Suggested Prayer: Dear Lord, how grateful we are for all the friends our family shares. Lord, we pray for those people who are alone with few or no friends. Comfort them, Lord. Help our family to reach out in kindness this week to such people. *Amen.*

MOVING DAY

OPENING PRAYER

God Our Father, it's so hard to move! It's hard to leave old friends and a place we've loved for a new, unknown area. Dearest Lord, be with us tonight as we share our thoughts and feelings about moving. Thank you, dear Lord, for this *Family Night. Amen.*

A SPECIAL NOTE FOR PARENTS

It's been said moving is most difficult for children between the ages of two and four, and for teenagers. Difficulties begin from seventh to ninth grade with ninth grade being especially hard, and then junior and senior years in high school are even more difficult. For infants to two years and children five years old to ten years old, there are few problems. For them a move can broaden their horizons and be a great adventure.

ACTIVITY TIME

Young Family

The Great Adventure. *Materials:* paper, crayons. Have Mom and Dad start with where they lived when they were first married and draw a house for each move the family has made up until the present. Then each person draw and color a picture of his favorite place to live and tell why. Answer together: Why is moving a great adventure?

Middle Years Family

Moving: Advantages and Disadvantages. *Materials:* paper and pens. Have each family member write a paragraph on how he feels about moving. Read them together. As a family discuss what are the advantages and disadvantages in moving. Then together list twenty of each on a large sheet of paper. Put it away for sometime in the future to be used if the family ever decides to move.

Adult Family

Scripture Time. *Materials:* Bible. Read aloud Matthew 8:18-22 and Luke 9:57-62. Share thoughts about these passages and moving. What was the most difficult move each ever made in the past? What move was the most fun? Share the reasons why for each.

SNACK

Try a "Black Cow"—root beer and ice cream soda.

ENTERTAINMENT

Take turns answering: If I had to move tomorrow, where would I move? If I could take only three possessions with me, what would they be?

SHARING

1. Share a joy from this week.
2. Each share a good quality about himself and the person to his right.
3. Share a moment someone felt very lonely.

CLOSING PRAYER

—Suggested Prayer: Dearest Lord, thank you for this *Family Night* and for the chance to share our feelings about moving. Lord, we pray for all the families who will move soon and ask your Spirit to comfort them when they say their good-byes. Grant them a safe journey to a new home and then, Lord, bless them with new loving relationships. Help them to understand you will always be there with them even if they feel lonely. *Amen.*

FLOWERS— GOD'S JEWELS OF SPRINGTIME

OPENING PRAYER

Oh wonderful Jesus, thank you for the magnificent beauty of springtime. Thank you for new life everywhere, fresh, lush and sweet smelling. Thank you for flowers and how they speak to us of you. Be with us this *Family Night*, dearest Jesus, and bless us as we gather in your name. *Amen.*

SOMETHING TO THINK ABOUT

Flowers are such a genuine reflection of God's beauty and grace. Every flower is a masterpiece of color, shape and texture. They are delicate and each so individualistic if one looks closely. The beauty and fragrance of flowers prick our hearts to joy, to love and even prayer. Flowers live fully today in total array and vulnerability. Flowers help God whisper to our souls, "Live fully, love totally, give completely."

ACTIVITY TIME

Young Family

Me, a flower? *Materials:* books or magazines with pictures of flowers; clever minds. Have each family member think of a flower he would choose to represent himself (example—a violet, shy and humble; a sunflower, vivacious and outgoing). Then choose a flower to represent each family member. Share together. Then pick or buy some fresh flowers to use as a centerpiece during the week.

Middle Years Family

Plant Nursery Visit. *Materials:* car and a wee bit of money. Take a trip to a plant nursery and examine all the varieties of flowers for sale. Notice the colors and shapes, shape of leaves. Plan to bring home a few and then plant them in a window box or the yard.

Adult Family

Scripture Time. *Materials:* Bible. Read aloud Matthew 6:28-34. Share your thoughts. Share an experience from the past about a favorite flower garden.

SNACK

Rainbow flavored sherbet ice cream sodas or fresh strawberry whipped cream pie (if strawberries are available).

ENTERTAINMENT

Take an early evening walk as a group and make a list of all the different signs of springtime the family sees.

SHARING

1. Each share his favorite flower and why.
2. Each share what he loves best about the month of May.
3. Someone share a moment he felt close to God recently.

CLOSING PRAYER

—Suggested Prayer: Oh Child Jesus, we praise you and ask that you teach us your ways of love and giving. Teach us your ways of openness and joy. We praise you little Child Jesus. Make us one in you. *Amen.*

YEAH! FOR MOMS!

OPENING PRAYER

Lord Jesus, thank you for our mom. She's terrific and we love her. Thank you for your mom too, Jesus, beautiful and gentle Mary. Be with us tonight, Lord, and help us to celebrate our mom. *Amen.*

ACTIVITY TIME

Young Family and Middle Years Family

"Mom is Queen Night." *Materials:* paper, crayons, tape and scissors. Cut out a crown for Mom to wear marked, "Yeah! for Mom!" Also cut out a big heart to pin on her dress listing the family names with "You're Wonderful" in bright letters in the center. Plan a party with small gifts or good deeds written on papers. Be sure to cook the dinner and do the dishes for her tonight.

Adult Family

"Mom You're Special." Plan a dinner out and a corsage for her as a surprise.

SNACK

Bake a cake and decorate it "In Honor of_____, Our Great Mom."

ENTERTAINMENT

Plan a "This is Your Life" for Mom, starting with her childhood and continuing up to the present.

SHARING

1. Each person (except Mom) share their favorite time with her over the past year.
2. Each share a moment of fun from last week.
3. Share when someone felt God's presence in a special way.

CLOSING PRAYER

—Suggested Prayer: Gentle Jesus, thank you for this evening and for our dearest mother. Thank you for her love and the hours of labor she spends caring for all of us. But most of all, Jesus, help us to show our love for her through our helpfulness and cheerfulness and our hugs and kisses. *Amen.*

PENTECOST— WIND AND FIRE

OPENING PRAYER

Come Holy Spirit and fill the hearts of your faithful, and enkindle in us the fire of your love. Make us, mold us, into a family exploding with LIFE! *Amen.*

SOMETHING TO THINK ABOUT

Pentecost is the day the Spirit comes in fire and wind. It didn't just happen all those years ago but continues daily. When we see Christ's love and are filled with it, we become immersed in the life of the Spirit. It is a glowing, living thing that must shine forth and must act.

ACTIVITY TIME

Young Family

Drama Time. *Materials:* people, costumes (optional). Assign parts to all the family and then act out the story of the apostles in the Upper Room on Pentecost. After the play take turns sharing how each imagines the different apostles felt. Then try to think of ways in which the Spirit is a part of our daily lives and also present in the life of the Church today. Make a list of 7 of them and put it on the refrigerator for the coming week before Pentecost Sunday.

Middle Years Family

Blow, Wind, Blow. *Materials:* Bible, an electric hair dryer. Use the hair dryer and blow it on each person's face. Share some thoughts about wind—soft breezes, winter winds, even tornadoes or hurricanes. Can anyone think why the Holy Spirit is compared to the wind? Share ideas. Then read aloud John 3:5-8.

Adult Family

Scripture Time. *Materials:* Bible. Read aloud Acts 2:1-11 and 1 Corinthians 12:3-7 and John 20:19-23. Does the Spirit come in fire and wind today? Share a possible personal experience with the Spirit.

SNACK AND ENTERTAINMENT

Take a trip to a nearby park. Make a fire and have a marshmallow roast.

SHARING

Gather in a circle and:

1. Take turns sharing a good quality you recognize in the person to the left of you in the circle.
2. Take turns seeing how long each person can hold his breath. What force is it that forces us to breathe again?

CLOSING PRAYER

The Lord's Prayer.

MEMORIAL DAY

Theme: A Time to Remember

OPENING PRAYER

Our Heavenly Father, bless this evening as our family gathers in your presence to share, to love, to listen and to learn from one another. Thank you, Lord, for our family—unique and important in your eyes. Keep us ever open to your message of love and help us to spread your presence to all we meet this coming week. Thank you, Father, for our *Family Night. Amen.*

SOMETHING TO THINK ABOUT

Memorial Day has for a long time served as a cue to our nation to welcome summer and by tradition has been a day for remembering the past. Often it is a day that families visit cemeteries and leave flowers at the graves of loved ones. Memorial Day also reminds our families of the men who died for our country in wars and speaks to us of the ideals that are worth dying for. It's a time to reflect on the lives of our loved ones who have died. What were their dreams, hopes, struggles? How do they influence us today? Let's share tonight.

ACTIVITY TIME

Young Family

Heroes Worth Remembering. *Materials:* paper, crayons, string, pencils. Each make a small booklet about his or her favorite hero, living or dead. Plan to take some time talking about what kinds of people can be heroes. Through pictures and writing share about the hero. Lastly, each explain why he chose that particular hero. Use the booklets as a centerpiece at mealtime during the coming week.

Middle Years Family

To Remember is Important. Find some old pictures and keepsakes of family members who have died. Share what was important to him or her. Share a funny story about them and then make a list of 5 positive ways they influence our family today.

Adult Family

Scripture Time. Read aloud from the Bible Micah 4:3-4 or John 6:47-58 or Lamentations 5. Share thoughts on what they say to us about Memorial Day.

SNACK

Try a baked blueberry pie or grandma's or great-grandma's family recipe treat.

ENTERTAINMENT

"We Remember Who?" As a group take turns guessing in 20 questions or less the name of a famous person one family member has chosen from the past. Be sure each person has a chance to be "it."

SHARING

1. Each share a favorite memory about a dead relative or friend.
2. Share what each is most looking forward to next week.
3. Someone share a moment he felt especially important last week.

CLOSING PRAYER

—Suggested Prayer: Holy Spirit of God, we praise you and honor you in our family.

God the Father, we pray for all those who have died in our family and those who have died in war.

Lord Jesus Christ, thank you for becoming man and teaching us the way to the Father, through the Spirit. *Amen.*

WELCOME, SUMMER TIME

OPENING PRAYER

Dearest Lord, this summertime beckons our family to grow in so many unknown ways. Lord, be our guide this summer. Help us to be helpful and joyful, witnessing your love first to one another in our family, then to others. Jesus, be with us in a special way this *Family Night. Amen.*

LESSON: *Use one of the following formats*

Young Family

Materials: one large piece of cardboard, old magazines, scissors, glue and crayons. Together make a mural entitled "Summertime Is" covering the cardboard with some appealing summertime scenes or activities. After the mural is filled write in the center in crayon "Summertime Is." Each person shares his thoughts on what this summer can mean to him.

Middle Years Family

Materials: paper, pencils. Have each family member write two paragraphs: the first, what he likes best about summer and the second, what he likes least about summer. Share them all together. Then together make a list of five ideas for making this summer a delight for everyone.

Adult Family

Materials: pencils, paper. Together make a weekly chart with jobs listed for different family members. Plan to rotate them weekly for the summer. Then each person can make a list of four inexpensive things he'd like to do this summer with the family. Write them on small pieces of paper and then place them in a bowl for the family to draw from periodically during the summer months.

SNACK

Fresh fruit in season.

ENTERTAINMENT

Play a favorite family game. Try to avoid watching TV.

SHARING

1. Each share a moment you were happy this past week.
2. Each share a time when you felt left out; what were your feelings?
3. Each share a moment when you felt close to God.

CLOSING PRAYER

—Scripture: Psalm 65:5-19

—Group Spontaneous Prayer

—Suggested prayer: Dearest Jesus, thank you for this evening. We each love you, Jesus, and we ask you to heal any hurts within us. Help us, Jesus, to be a more loving and thoughtful family during this summer. *Amen.*

TIME—HOW WE CHANGE

OPENING PRAYER

Dearest Father, how each of us is changing as we pass along on our life's journey. We hardly seem the same person we were five or ten years ago; our body changes, our mind changes and our spirit changes. Yet, Lord, each of us is essentially the same person and indeed every one of us is a mystery. Oh, Father, thank you for making us the wonder that we are and thank you for your presence with us yesterday, today and tomorrow. We love you, Father. *Amen.*

ACTIVITY TIME

Young Family

Life Line. *Materials:* paper, crayons, pencils. Each draw a line across a sheet of paper to represent his life with the date of his birth on one end and today's date on the other. Choose four places along the life line that each one thinks he changed significantly. Mark them along the line with the date and why each was chosen. All share their life line with the family.

Middle Years Family

Future Telling. *Materials:* none. Take about a minute of silence to

think about the future five years from now. Take turns pretending it's five years from now, and complete the statements:

1. I live . . .
2. I work or go to school at . . .
3. My favorite clothes outfit is . . .
4. I have traveled . . .
5. My faith situation is . . .

Adult Family

Scripture Time. *Materials:* Bible. Read together Ephesians 4:17-24 and 1 Peter 4:1-11. How do these readings apply to our family?

SNACK

Pop some corn and take note of how it changes.

ENTERTAINMENT

(Choose a *very* dark room.) One person closes his eyes and counts to 30. Others hide about the room, keep silent and freeze at the count of 30. The person who is "it" feels about the room, keeping eyes closed, until he touches all the people. The first person touched is "it" for the next round. It's great fun!

SHARING

1. Each share a moment from the past week when he felt especially joyful.
2. Share a happy memory from 2 years ago.
3. Tell a fun story from 4 years ago, if you can remember.

CLOSING PRAYER

—Suggested Prayer: Dearest Father, thank you for our sharings this evening. Thank you for helping us discover the many ways we each change with time. Bless us this week, Father, and may we spend our time wisely. *Amen.*

THANK YOU, GOD, FOR DADS

OPENING PRAYER

Dear Heavenly Father, thank you so much for dads. They make our days complete with their presence. Bless fathers everywhere, dear Lord, but especially bless ours tonight. Let this be a very special *Family Night. Amen.*

LESSON

Young Family

Materials: colored paper, crayons, scissors, and glue. Make a paper crown for Dad to wear, decorate it with special words describing

Dad, then make a large paper button saying, "We Love Dad." Then have Dad wear both of them. Next, each person draw a picture or short letter sharing the happiest time he or she spent with Dad this past year. Dad, himself, can write on "Why He Likes Being a Dad." Then everyone share, together, their letters or pictures and make a folder for Dad to keep the sharings in so he can look at them during the summer.

Middle Years Family

Materials: poster board, pencils, crayons or magic markers. Make a large poster together entitled "Our Dad Is . . ." Then present it to Dad; it may be hung in the meal area for the week. Then have a "We Appreciate Dad" time; each person takes a turn to tell Dad: (1) the single thing you admire most about Dad and why, (2) what is one of Dad's greatest accomplishments, (3) the funniest thing you ever saw Dad do, (4) something that you are grateful to Dad for doing for you.

Adult Family

Materials: Bible. Read aloud Romans 8:14-17 or Ephesians 3:14, 15 or Matthew 6:25-34. Share your thoughts on God as our Father. Each take a turn sharing his favorite memory about his own Dad.

SNACK

Pop some popcorn; make "Black Cows"—vanilla ice cream and root beer.

ENTERTAINMENT

Play a game of hide and seek. (Be sure to set boundaries.)

SHARING

1. Each share a time you felt especially loved during the past week.
2. Share a moment in which you were proud of a particular accomplishment.
3. Share a moment when you felt excluded or left out.
4. Share a time when you felt close to God.

CLOSING PRAYER

—Spontaneous Prayer

—Lord's Prayer

—Suggested prayer: Dear Heavenly Father, how grateful our family is for sharing tonight together. Thank you, Father, for creating families where we can care, grow, sometimes disagree, but most of all, love one another. Thank you, too, Father for our Dad. *Amen.*

CRITICISM IS A NASTY WORM

OPENING PRAYER

Gentle Jesus, come, Lord Jesus, and be with us this *Family Night*. Help us to build each other up, not tear one another down. Help our family to smile rather than to frown. *Amen*.

OPENING POEM

Criticism

Criticism is a nasty worm
That eats away
At our nice home.

It chews away day and night
Munching, crunching every bite.
Soon our home is filled with gloom
For laughter or love can find no room.

LESSON

Young Family

Materials: paper plates, crayons, pieces of string or yarn. Each person colors a smiling face on a paper plate. On the back side color a frowning face. Then punch a hole in the top and loop the yarn or string through the hole and tie it. Take turns sharing phrases that are sometimes said that make us happy or sad; for example, shut up!, you're lovely, I hate you, that's a good job. Try to discover some special phrases that are peculiar to your own family. As different phrases are shared, turn the faces to show each person's reactions. Put the faces near the meal area and before dinner, have each person share which side of the face best depicts how he feels.

Middle Years Family

Materials: dictionary, paper, pens, shoe box, aluminum foil. Together cover the shoe box with foil and then mark it on each side, "The Criticism Box." Set aside. Each write a definition of the word criticism. Share together, then look it up in a dictionary and read the definition aloud. Then discuss what the family can do to reduce criticism at home. Each write two ideas and place them in the "Criticism Box." Keep the box on the dinner table and each night draw one of the papers and read it aloud.

Adult Family

Materials: Bible. Read aloud Romans 14:13. Share your thoughts. Each take a turn sharing two stories from the past: (1) a time when, because of fear of criticism, you failed to do something you really wanted to do; (2) a time when, because you were supported and encouraged, you were able to accomplish something you never dreamed of being able to do.

SNACK

Make Happy Face sundaes: ice cream, with raisins for a nose and mouth, and cherries for eyes.

ENTERTAINMENT

Name Game: place someone in the center blindfolded; the group chooses one person to describe to the blindfolded person in three words or less another individual in the family. The person in the center sees if he can guess within the three tries. Try to make the words difficult for older children and easy for younger ones. Be sure to use only words of praise or good things about the person.

SHARING IDEAS

1. Each share what your feelings are like when you are told "I love you."
2. Share a struggle from the past week.
3. Share a favorite book and why you like it.

CLOSING PRAYER

—Spontaneous Prayer

—Scripture: Matthew 7:7, 8

—Suggested prayer: Dear Jesus, thank you for tonight. Bless your families everywhere but especially those families that are suffering from want of food or shelter or are in need of kindness or love. Praise you, Lord Jesus. *Amen.*

CLOSING POEM

Criticism is a nasty worm
That eats away
At our nice home.

We can stop him eating here
With words of kindness, words of cheer.
Soon our home dances with joy
Filling with love each girl and boy.

OPENING PRAYER

Oh, Lord, hooray for you for making our family and all your families across our great country. Lord, help us to appreciate the goodness of our country. Help us to work at improving it where it needs help. Bless our president and all his family. Thanks for this *Family Night*, Lord. *Amen.*

LESSON

Young Family

Materials: crepe paper (red, white and blue), crayons, plain paper, family bikes, wagons or strollers. Decorate the vehicles with crepe paper; plan on having a children's block parade on the morning of the 4th. Set the time and then make invitations to deliver around the block. Plan to have Kool-Aid ready for parade participants at the end of the morning. Deliver the invitations as a family.

Middle Years Family

Materials: plain paper, pens. Pass out scrap paper and have each person divide his paper in two columns; then number one to seven in each column. At the top of one column mark what you believe are some of our nation's successes. In the other column write our nation's failures. Start with 1900 to 1910 with No. 1, then 1910 to 1920 and so on. You might want to refresh one another on our nation's history before starting. Then compare papers. Together compose a prayer for our country to be said nightly or on July 4th.

Adult Family

Materials: Bible, writing paper, pens. Read aloud Romans 13:1-7. Share thoughts about it and our nation's government. Each write a short letter of encouragement to your state senators or congressmen.

SNACK

Pink lemonade and a homemade fruit pie.

ENTERTAINMENT

Play some favorite records and see which family member can come up with the most unusual dance step. Or Mom and Dad can teach some old steps.

SHARING

1. What was your most favorite 4th of July over the past five years? Describe it.
2. Share a moment each person felt especially close to another family member.
3. Someone share a time he felt God's presence.

CLOSING PRAYER

—Scripture: 2 Chronicles 7:14.

—Suggested prayer: Oh Lord, thank you for our beautiful country with its great mountains, rivers, open plains, and forests. Help our people to treasure and protect this country's natural beauty. Thank you, too, for our freedoms of speech, of the press, and of religion. Lord, bless our country this coming year. *Amen.*

VACATION FOLLY

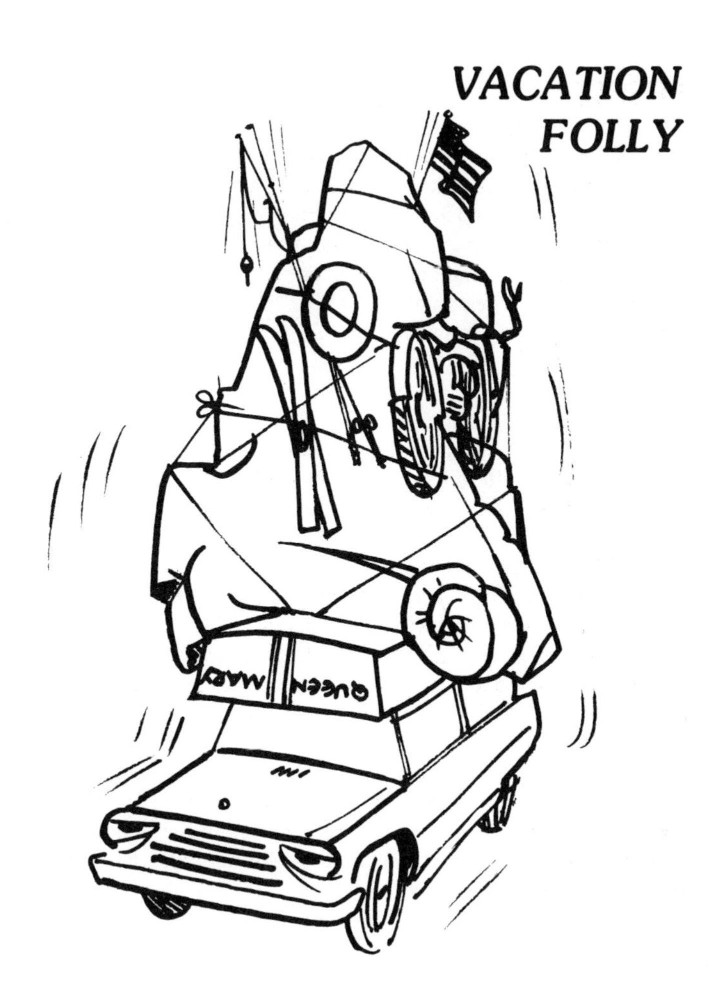

OPENING PRAYER

Dearest Lord, hurrah, hurrah, it's vacation time! Bless us, Lord, during this vacation and protect us on our trip whether it be near or far from home. Thank you for all the fun we are anticipating together. Be with us, Lord, and share our joy. *Amen.*

LESSON

Young Family

Materials: crayons, tape, colored tissue or aluminum foil, small cardboard box for each family member. The small boxes are for each family member to keep in the car for his special little things; examples: tiny trucks, crayons, paper dolls, cigarettes, gum, facial tissue, wash 'n dries, camera, film, small radio. Decorate the boxes with the tissue or foil and have each person mark his box *"[Name]'s Special Box."* Each take a turn finishing this sentence, "As a result of this vacation, I want my family to . . ."

Middle Years Family

Materials: pencils, paper, dictionary. "Everyone has needs." Each family member write a list of what he wishes to experience from the family vacation. Examples: rest, excitement, see relatives, learn some history, enjoy nature, grow closer as a family. After everyone shares his NEEDS, integrate them and make a priority list for the vacation for the whole family. Then each make a list of five ways fights usually start *in the family.* Each read his list to the family. Then combine the lists to five. Each person write after each point, one way to minimize its occurrence. Share. Take the list on the vacation to refer to. "Good luck."

Adult Family

Materials: pencils, paper, Bible. Each list what his goal is for the vacation, and how much money the family can afford to spend for the vacation. Plan how the goals can be kept within the budget. Look up "vacation" in the dictionary. Share thoughts about its definition. Read aloud Psalm 90:12 and Ephesians 5:15, 16.

SNACK

Cupcakes and soda.

ENTERTAINMENT (Ideas for a Car Trip)

1. "I See It" game; decide on something to watch for—examples: cows, tractors, horses, Volkswagens. Whoever sees it first gets a point.

2. Memorize a poem or Scripture passage.
3. Alphabet game—I came from A (complete as the name of a town) with a truck load of B (complete as the name of a fruit, vegetable or animal) and my name is C (complete as a person's first name). The next family member continues with D for the name of his town, E for his fruit, etc., and so on through the alphabet.
4. One person reads a story.
5. Hold a songfest.

For families with small children, plan a lot of stops along the way and take along extra little snacks.

SHARING

1. Share a high point from last week.
2. Share a very important moment with a friend.
3. Share a time you felt lonely.

CLOSING PRAYER

—Spontaneous Prayer

—Psalm 39:4-7

—Suggested prayer: Dearest Jesus, thank you for tonight, but even more, thank you for vacations. They give us time to relax, to love, to enjoy and to be together as a family. Thank you, dearest Jesus. We love you. *Amen.*

va·ca·tion - a respite, intermission, rest, recess –

FITNESS FOR GOD'S TEMPLES

OPENING PRAYER

Holy Spirit, fill our family this evening with your presence. Help us to treasure one another and help to keep us all in shape, especially physically. *Amen.*

LESSON

(Scripture—1 Corinthians 3:16, 17)

Young Family

Materials: an inexpensive tape measure, construction paper, crayons, photos of family members, glue or scotch tape. Mount the tape measure on construction paper and print at the top "God's Special Temples." Measure and record the height of family members, and write their names next to their height. Along the side of the construction paper, place individual pictures. For taller family members, place their pictures and heights near the top. Hang this chart on the inside of a closet or pantry door and when school begins, measure everyone again to see if any "temples" have grown.

Middle Years Family

Materials: Bible, paper, pens or crayons. Read aloud 1 Cor 3:16, 17. What is it saying to us as individuals, and as a family? Share and discuss what different family members can do to keep physically fit. What about grooming habits, exercise habits and eating habits? Choose two areas for improvement and work out a schedule for the coming week for exercise.

Adult Family

Materials: Bible, scale. Read aloud 1 Cor 3:16, 17. Share thoughts about it. How fit are the family members? Are there any members overweight? Take turns using the scale. (Weight doesn't have to be shared.) Do we have an obligation to God to keep our

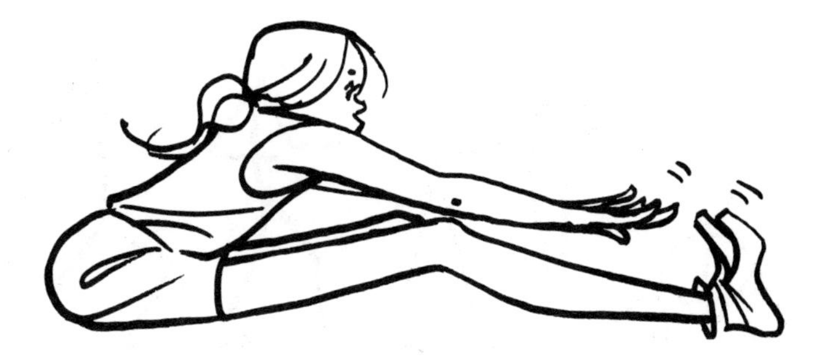

bodies fit? Share thoughts on good balanced diets and also practical ways to lose weight. No one should be made to feel pressured to lose weight, nor should one family member criticize any overweight condition of another family member.

SNACK

Fresh fruits in season.

ENTERTAINMENT

Celebrate one family member: share a "This is Your Life" with photos from babyhood, recall special important events and make a button to wear—his name and "we love you."

SHARING

1. Each share a moment you felt at peace inside.
2. Each share a time you felt hassled or rushed.
3. Each share a moment you felt especially close to another family member.

CLOSING PRAYER

—Spontaneous Prayer

—Suggested prayer: Thank you wondrous Lord for making us temples of your Holy Spirit. Thank you for your plan for each of our lives. Help us to be open to you and to listen to your words within our hearts. Thank you for this *Family Night. Amen.*

HURRAH FOR GRAND-PARENTS

OPENING PRAYER

Our Father in Heaven, how grateful we are for being able to share this evening as a family. Tonight we pray especially for our grandparents and ask you to bless them in a very special way. Thank you, Father, for making grandparents for us to learn from and for us to love. St. Joachim and St. Ann, pray for us. *Amen.*

LESSON

Young Family

(If grandparents are in town, have them over for dinner and an evening of "Honor Grandparents." Share little gifts, their favorite treat, balloons, big red hearts to wear with "Hurrah for Grandma ____________ and Grandpa ____________" on them.) For families whose grandparents are not in the same town or are deceased: materials: photos of grandparents, writing paper, pens, crayons, telephone. Share different pictures of grandparents, even some pictures of great-grandparents, if available. Share some fun stories together about the grandparents. Each person write a letter or draw a picture saying how very dear and very much they are loved. Plan to mail them tomorrow. Telephone grandparents later in the evening and let each family member have a chance to visit.

Middle Years Family

(If grandparents are in town). Have them over and prepare an "Honor Grandparents Night." Plan a "this is your life" and share all sorts of fun information about them. Try to make it a surprise if possible. If they're out of town mail them a "thank you letter" from the family for being terrific grandparents.

Adult Family

Materials: Bible. Read aloud Deuteronomy 4:9 and 2 Timothy 1:5. Recall some old stories about grandparents. What is so different about life today? If you could change one thing today, what would it be?

SNACK

Watermelon or a grandparent's favorite dessert.

ENTERTAINMENT

Hold a watermelon-seed spitting contest.

SHARING

1. Share a time someone felt super-happy during the last week.
2. Share a moment when someone was really sad.
3. Share a time someone felt God's presence in a comforting way.

CLOSING PRAYER

Dearest Lord Jesus, praise you, wondrous Jesus! Bless us as we strive to serve you daily. Help us to continue to grow in your love. Thank you for tonight and for our grandparents. St. Joachim and St. Ann, (grandparents) of our Lord Jesus, pray for our families. *Amen.*

THE FAMILY BANK

OPENING PRAYER

Father, be present as we come together to celebrate our *Family Night*. We thank you for the many resources that are at our disposal. Help us to use them wisely and generously, especially in service to others. *Amen.*

SOMETHING TO THINK ABOUT

We hear a lot these days about limited natural resources, about saving and conserving, about using resources wisely. Family life can be viewed that way, too. We have "x" number of material things and there are a certain number of people who make up our family unit. Let us look at the goods that we have, the services that we render and how we use our resources.

Services are very important resources in many ways, even more important than material goods. Consider the kinds of services we can render to each other and to others outside our family too.

ACTIVITY TIME

Young Family

Find a bank (a box or jar will do) and draw pictures of the major family resources—house, cars, bikes, etc. Deposit in the bank and talk about the following points: How do we care for the things we have? What conservation tips can we share with one another?

Middle Years Family

Make a family service chart listing the jobs that need to be done around the house and ways in which we can be of service to some specific other people. Let each member sign up for the ones he will be responsible for. Erase periodically and sign up for different ones.

Write down one thing you will do to add to the Family Bank. Tell the family what it is while you deposit it in the bank. Chips can be used in place of slips of paper to symbolize the services promised.

Adult Family

Each individual makes a list of the things he needs to get along. Go through the list a second time and put a * next to each item that you absolutely cannot get along without, thereby separating needs from wants. Have each person read his revised list of needs only. Rank your top three major needs by placing number "1" next to the most important, etc.

Everyone puts into the bank according to ability and receives according to his needs. When you are young you are mostly at the receiving end but as you grow older you have greater possibilities for giving. Read and discuss Acts of the Apostles 2:42-47. How is your family like the early Christian communities?

SNACK

Even small children can help make no-bake cookies, for a cookies-and-milk or hot-cocoa treat.

ENTERTAINMENT

Try pitching pennies into a milk carton decorated to look like your Family Bank. Back up a step each time to make the game more challenging.

SHARING

1. Share the greatest resource your family has, the one that is most important to you.
2. Share one way in which you can contribute to the family bank.
3. Share what you think would happen if everyone kept taking out but no one put anything in.

CLOSING PRAYER

Build your prayer by each person completing one of the following:

God, our Father, we
Praise You for . . .
Thank You for . . .
Are *Sorry* for . . .
Ask You for . . .
Amen.

MEALTIME TOGETHER

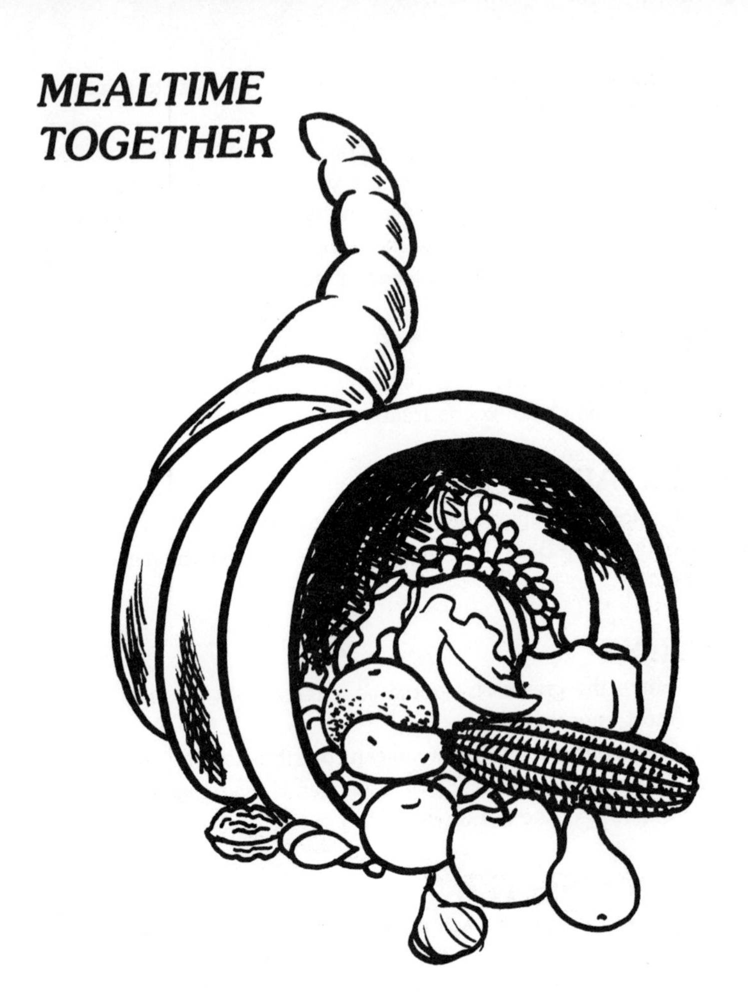

OPENING PRAYER

Dear Jesus, whenever people come together to share or celebrate there almost always is a meal. How wise you are, Lord Jesus, in giving us yourself in the Eucharistic meal. Thank you for tonight, Lord Jesus, and also for our family gatherings at mealtime. *Amen.*

LESSON

Young Family

Materials: poster board, crayons, magazines, scissors, glue. Divide the poster into four sections. Mark them: (1) meat, (2) milk, (3) vegetables and fruits, (4) breads and cereals. Mark at the top "Good Eating for Our Family." Color or cut out pictures of food to fit into the four categories. For good health: milk—3 glasses for kids; 2 glasses for adults; meat—2 or more servings; vegetables and fruits—4 or more servings; bread and cereals—4 or more servings daily. Look back over today. Have everyone list and evaluate what he or she ate today. Put the poster on the refrigerator.

Middle Years Family

Materials: paper, crayons. "Mealtime Memories." Each person takes about two minutes to recall what their dinner table was like

when they were kindergarten age. Color a picture of the table, where each person sat; make colors for the mood of the different people. Share pictures and explain them. Answer together, what are mealtimes like now in the family? Review the past week; how many meals were shared together? Is mealtime a hassle or is it pleasant? How can the mealtime together be improved? List three ways for the coming week. Try them.

Adult Family

Materials: Bible. Read aloud Gen 18:1-9, then John 21:9-14. Why a meal in these readings? What are they saying? Plan a family reach-out: have a pot luck dinner for some neighbors or a single person. Set a date and plan the meal.

SNACK

Say "No snack tonight." What are the family reactions? Okay—hot fudge sundaes!

ENTERTAINMENT

Stage a water-balloon tossing contest.

SHARING

1. Share a time someone wanted a particular thing to eat and he finally got it.
2. Each person share what is his favorite thing to eat, and what he hates to eat.
3. Share a moment someone felt close to God.

CLOSING PRAYER

Gentle Jesus, we thank you for our *Family Night* this evening. Jesus, how well you understand families and how we need to come together and share. Thank you for food and how it can draw us together at mealtime. Jesus, we pray for those who don't have enough food and for those who are actually starving. Strengthen them, Jesus, for that terrible nightmare and burden. *Amen.*

LISTENING

OPENING PRAYER

Sweet Child Jesus, where are you? Help us to learn to listen when you call. Through listening we will hear your voice in nature; listening, we will hear your whisper in the wind; listening, we will hear you in the laughter of children. Oh, yes, Jesus, help us to learn to listen; help us to learn to hear when you speak. *Amen.*

LESSON

Young Family

Materials: NONE. All go outside in the backyard or a nearby park and sit together for five minutes, silently and listen to all the sounds. Then share all the different kinds of noises each person heard. Then finish these sentences:

1. It is most difficult for me to listen when . . .
2. It is very easy for me to listen when . . .
3. My favorite time of listening is . . .
4. When I know someone is listening to me I feel . . .

Middle Years Family

Materials: paper, pencils. Gather in a circle to play "pass the message." One person makes up a short message and whispers it to the next person until it completes the circle. The last person repeats it out loud. How has the message changed? Give three examples, in the family, of how this has happened. Each write out five times when it is hard for him to listen. Each person list five ways he can improve his listening abilities. Share lists. Choose two for the whole family to work at during the week, write them in big letters, and put them on the refrigerator door.

Adult Family

Materials: pencil, paper. Each person recalls someone he knew who was a good listener. List why; try to write at least four reasons. Share on paper the written efforts. Each person nameshthe single greatest reason that it is hard for him to listen at a particular time. Write a paragraph about why it is more difficult to listen than to talk? Read aloud and share.

SNACK

Homemade popsicles; listen to how different people eat theirs.

ENTERTAINMENT

Take a walk around the block. Listen to all the different types of noises.

SHARING

1. Share a time one felt listened to during the past week.
2. Share a moment when someone felt close to God.
3. Share a favorite experience.

CLOSING PRAYER

Sweet Child Jesus, help our family to become better listeners to one another. Jesus, keep our telephone a servant to us; let us not be slaves to it. Help us to have quiet times so we may listen to your soft voice and, thus, be able to share your *messages* with others. *Amen.*

For Mom and Dad and Anybody Else

Listening to our children demands restraint on our part from:

1. *Interrupting*
2. *Over-reacting*
3. *Criticizing*

Listening to our children teaches them to listen to others.

Listening to our children gives them a sense of self-worth, and it teaches them to be able to express themselves.

To listen well demands:

1. *Practice!!!*
2. *Concentration!!!!*
3. *Love!!!!!*

SUMMERTIME RE-CAP

OPENING PRAYER

Thank you, dear Lord, for summertime. Thank you for its good fruits, the music of rain showers, desert dust devils that dash across the open plains, and warm, clear, star-filled nights. Thank you, too, for smiling children's faces and for unselfish parents. Thank you now and always for your gift of love. *Amen.*

Dear Friends in Christ,

For most of us families the next few weeks will bring the fall school rush. The lazy summer of fun is about to end, and new schedules will begin for kids and adults. A new season will be unfolding; whether it be first grade, tenth grade, or college, there will be an aura of anticipation and excitement. For parents and for families without children the neighborhood will be suddenly quiet. (Thee will be moments of reflection, for time again is passing.) Tonight as we close this small booklet of Family Night *fun, let us pause in thanksgiving for "summertime."*

The Reillys

LESSON

Young Family

Materials: construction paper, notebook, paper, crayons, glue or scotch tape, one piece of yarn. Make a "Family Summer Memory Book." Put in special dates of outings, fun moments, ticket stubs, funny stories, each person's height and weight (Mom and Dad, too), and one thing each would like to do next summer. Save it to look at next May.

Middle Years Family

Materials: daily calendar, paper, pencils. Look back over the summer months. Everyone chooses his favorite moment, day, or week during the summer. If all could share the summer again, would the family do anything different? What? What was the funniest thing that happened this summer? The worst thing? Take turns sharing. Make a list of things the family would like to do next summer. Put away until next May.

Adult Family

Materials: poster board, pens. Make a poster with two columns for lists: one column for good deeds accomplished by each person or the family together; second column, ways God was present in the family over the next summer. (Examples: prayers answered, special moments, nature experiences). Place it near a family gathering place. Entitle the poster, "God lives with the __________ (family name) __________"

SNACK

Taffy apples, or apple crisp.

ENTERTAINMENT

Hold a "story-make-up." Have someone start a make-believe story, talk for one minute, have each family member add to it. Anything can happen!

SHARING IDEAS

1. Take turns sharing what the favorite time of day is for each person.
2. Each share one thing he is especially looking forward to this coming fall.
3. Each share a moment he felt loved.

CLOSING PRAYER

—Scripture: Romans 11:33-36

—Spontaneous Prayer

—Suggested prayer: Lord, prepare our family for the fresh adventure of this fall season. Help us to be aware of your presence in this time of transition. Thank you, dearest Lord, for this past summer and for the growth and awareness it has brought to us all. Thank you, too, for our *Family Nights. Amen.*

THE LEARNING TREE

OPENING PRAYER

God, our Great Teacher, you taught us through Jesus to be open to learning and growing. As we look ahead to a new school year, help us to be excited about all the learning opportunities that come our way. Send your Spirit to be with our family tonight and to be our Guide in all our learning adventures. *Amen.*

ACTIVITY TIME

Young Family

Take the children outside and find a tree, preferably a fruit tree. Let them simply explore the tree in every way possible: climb it, feel it, taste the fruit, examine the leaves. Talk about what the tree needs to grow and how it grows and changes, what the tree gives to us in its fruit, shade and beauty.

Middle Years Family

Materials: large sheet of paper, pencils, crayons. Do the activity described in "Young Family" section or obtain a copy of *The Giving Tree* by Sil Silverstein at your library or bookstore. Read it together and talk about the many ways the tree shared itself with others. Learning happens because people share with one another—what they know, who they are and what they can do. Make an outline of a tree on a large sheet of paper. Draw pictures of things that you can do that can be shared with others such as riding a skateboard, swimming, biking, etc.

Adult Family

Materials: Bible. Read aloud Luke 2:51, 52 which makes reference to Jesus growing in wisdom, age and grace. Also read Luke 4:16-22 where Jesus teaches Who He is.

How do we share who we are with each other? Tell about a time when you taught another something because you shared yourself, something you knew or a skill you have.

SNACK

A cool, refreshing summer drink.

ENTERTAINMENT

Play Family Fish Pond having children fish for their school supplies, pencils, notebooks, erasers, lunch boxes, etc. Use a yardstick, string and clothespin for the pole. A large box or sheet across a doorway can serve as the pond.

SHARING

1. Share a time when you learned something difficult.
2. Share how you feel about going to school.
3. Share the high point and low point of summer.

CLOSING PRAYER

—Suggested Prayer: Father, help us to be like Jesus, willing to share ourselves and our gifts so that others may learn. Thanks for the chance to share and grow with our family tonight. Bless all families everywhere. *Amen.*

LABOR DAY

Theme: Creation Continues

OPENING PRAYER

God our Creator, you made us man in your image and likeness and invited us to be your partners in continuing the work of creation. Your Son Jesus worked as a carpenter and taught us the dignity of hard work. Send your Spirit to make us alive to continuing creation as we celebrate Labor Day. *Amen.*

ACTIVITY TIME

Labor is continuing the act of creation. In creation God makes the world for us. By our labors we preserve, develop and wisely use these created gifts.

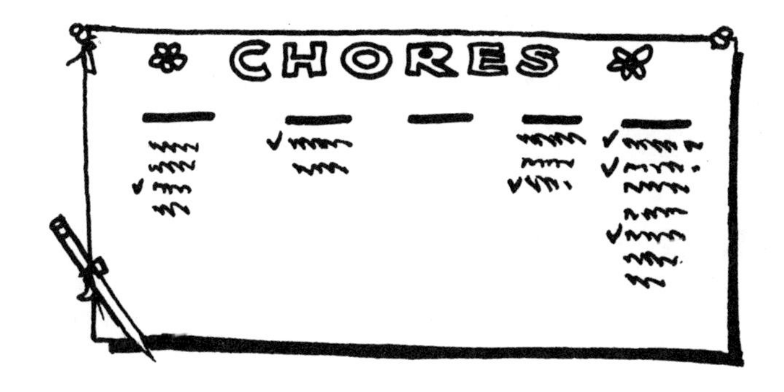

Young Family

In today's society many children have no idea of what their fathers and/or mothers do when they go off to work. Ideally, a trip to the place of work would be a good way to celebrate Labor Day sharing your work with your children. If that is impractical, try to re-create your work experience by using pictures from magazines or drawing a few illustrations as you tell about what you do.

Middle Years Family

Materials: paper or poster board, marking pens, scissors. Talk about the work that needs to be done around the house to make a happy family. Design a Chore Chart that lists all the tasks that need to be done. Design it in such a way that the names can be moved around occasionally. After the discussion let everyone make a name card and place it next to the chore they would choose to do. Designate how long these assignments will last and then change them around.

Adult Family

Have each working member of the family tell about his or her job, how it's done, what is enjoyable about it and some of the difficulties involved.

If you could do any kind of work, what would it be? Share your choices and tell why you would like to do that job.

SNACK

A treat of fresh fruit, a gift of creation. Make different kinds of clown faces, using fresh fruit.

ENTERTAINMENT

Play "I'm Thinking of a Worker and it begins with . . . (letter of the alphabet)." The person who guesses gets to be the next player.

SHARING

1. Share how you feel when the house is all messy.
2. Share how you feel when you walk into a neat and clean house.
3. Share a time when you were really surprised about something.

CLOSING PRAYER

—Suggested Prayer: Come Holy Spirit, fill the hearts of your faithful and enkindle in them the fire of your Divine Love. Send forth your Spirit and they shall be created and shall renew the face of the earth. *Amen.*

BON VOYAGE

OPENING PRAYER

Father, we praise you at the beginning of this new school year. Thank you for the adventure ahead, exploring your world, celebrating life as we travel together. Send your Spirit to be our guide as we plan our year's journey and embark upon our family adventure. *Amen.*

ACTIVITY TIME

Fall marks the beginning of a new year more clearly than New Year's Day, especially when there are school children involved. It is an ideal time to plan your family goals, to mark your calendar for special times and events, to decide how and when you will have your *Family Night.*

Young Family

Take a calendar—or make your own—and mark all the special occasions, birthdays, anniversaries, holidays, *Family Nights,* any other time to be reserved for family. If you design your own calendar, illustrate and decorate it colorfully and with meaningful symbols.

Middle Years and Adult Families

People who are going on a long trip often begin with a Bon Voyage Party. Sometimes a travel agent will give the group an idea of where they are going (your goals), how they are going to get there (your family activities), things to look forward to (celebrations of your family birthdays, anniversaries, holidays, etc.). Appoint someone to be your Travel Agent for the evening, the group leader. Plan your family goals. What would you like to accomplish this year together? How will you do it? Be sure your evening has a party tone. Make it fun!

SNACK

Party treats for the Bon Voyage Party: punch, nuts, candy.

ENTERTAINMENT

Try having a Family Talent Show. Each one could contribute something—a song, a joke or funny story, a trick.

SHARING

1. Share a hope or dream you have for your family.
2. Share one good way to improve your family life.
3. Share the high point of last year's family activities for you.

CLOSING PRAYER

—Suggested Prayer: Lord, bless our travels. Guide us as we embark on our "Bon Voyage" always aware of your Presence, ever growing in love and concern for each other. *Amen.*

PEOPLE ARE LIKE RAINBOWS

OPENING PRAYER

Dear Father, we praise and thank you for the rainbow of beautiful people in our lives. Help us to recognize the specialness of each one, especially those in our own family. *Amen.*

ACTIVITY TIME

People are like rainbows. They come in many colors and hues. They come into our lives and while they are there they fill it with color and beauty.

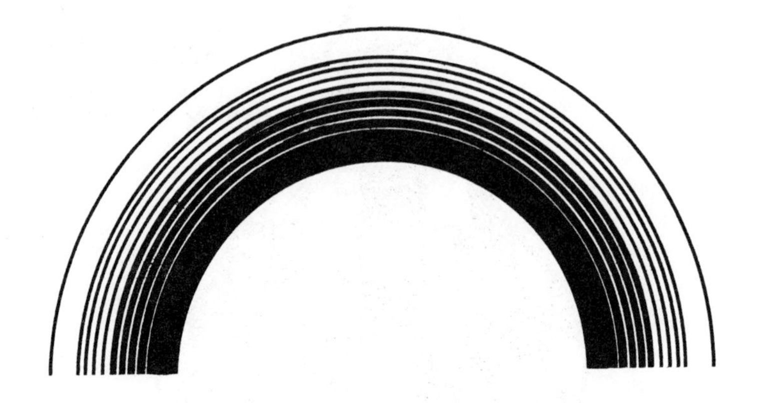

Young Family

Have fun playing with bubbles, commercial or homemade. Point out the rainbow of colors as the bubbles float through the air.

Middle Years Family

Rainbow Mobile. *Materials:* crayons, chalk, construction paper, string, hanger. Make a rainbow by cutting paper strips like arches. Use different colors. Each arch is suspended from a hanger by two pieces of string. The lengths of string are a little longer each time. Write the names of some of the new people, teachers and friends you have met since the new school year began.

Adult Family

Read the biblical story of Joseph and the Coat of Many Colors (Genesis, Chapters 37-47). Discuss the symbolism in the story and especially the family relationships—father/son, brothers/brothers. How do you deal with the dreams and aspirations of a family member? How do you handle jealousies, resentments, achievements and honors that occur in family life?

SNACK

A jello desert in a rainbow of colors would have to be prepared ahead of time. Rainbow sherbet or neopolitan ice cream would also carry out the theme quite well.

ENTERTAINMENT

Divide the family into two teams. Give each team a feather and see which side can keep the feather in the air the longest time by blowing it.

SHARING

1. Share something about the most beautiful person you know.
2. Share a time when you were jealous of another family member.
3. Share a time when you were really proud of someone in your family.

CLOSING PRAYER

—Join hands for spontaneous prayer.
—Suggested Prayer: The Prayer of St. Francis:

Lord, make me an instrument of your peace.
Where there is hatred, let me sow love;
where there is injury, pardon;
where there is doubt, faith;
where there is despair, hope;
where there is darkness, light.
O Divine Master,
grant that I may not so much seek to be consoled as to console;
to be understood as to understand;
to be loved as to love.
For it is in giving that we receive;
it is in pardoning that we are pardoned
and it is in dying that we are born to eternal life. Amen.

BEDTIME

OPENING PRAYER

Lord, help us to think about our day. How did we act at home? At school? At work? At play? Forgive us where we have failed. Help us to be more like Jesus in all that we do and say. *Amen.*

ACTIVITY TIME

Young Family

On this one evening plan an ideal bedtime. Some of the things you might do are: have a little wagon train made of people who move through the house and pick up toys and articles from daytime activities; serve a bedtime snack. Have everyone dress in pajamas and settle down in a soft, quiet, comfortable place. Share the good things of the day. Tell or read a favorite story and end with night prayers. This is a special time for hugs and good night kisses too.

Middle Years and Adult Families

Shut out the distractions and intrusions. Turn off the television and loud music and create a quiet atmosphere. Sit in a circle. Take turns naming a specific hour of the day. If one says "two o'clock" then each one shares what he or she was doing at that hour of the day. Complete the activity by having each one complete this sentence. "The best thing that happened to me today was . . . " Follow this by joining hands for spontaneous evening prayers or praying the Our Father together.

SNACK

Bedtime snacks of milk and crackers or cookies.

ENTERTAINMENT

Take turns telling your favorite bedtime story. You might consider using a few simple props and act it out or make a few simple finger puppets to enhance the tale.

SHARING

1. Share what you like to do most before going to bed.
2. Share the high point and low point of your day.
3. Share your happiest childhood memory associated with bedtime.

CLOSING PRAYER

—Spontaneous Prayer

—Suggested Prayer: Brother Jesus, when night came and the crowds went home, you closed the day with calm, peace and quiet in the presence of your Father. Gift us with your peace; quiet us at the end of each busy day so that we may be renewed. *Amen.*

OCTOBERFEST

OPENING PRAYER

Father, we observe the changes in nature—the leaves are turning colors, the squirrels are gathering acorns for the long winter ahead. Be with us as our family praises you in celebrating the glorious month of October. *Amen.*

ACTIVITY TIME

The Germanic people took special note of the arrival of October with the observance of the Octoberfest, an enjoyable way of marking the arrival of fall.

Young and Middle Years Families

Take a nature walk. Each member of the family has a small paper sack. As the family walks around the neighborhood collect signs of fall: leaves, seeds, etc. Upon your return gather around the table and make a collage either individually or as a family by gluing items in random fashion on a piece of cardboard. An alternative activity would be to use the items collected to make a fall centerpiece for the family table.

Adult Family

Print the verses taken from Psalm 65 on a large poster and illustrate it with pictures taken from magazines. An alternative is to illustrate it in scrapbook fashion, using magazine pictures.

"You have crowned the year with your bounty,
and your paths overflow with a rich harvest.
The untilled meadows overflow with it,
and rejoicing clothes the hills.
The fields are garmented with flocks,
and the valleys blanketed with grain.
They shout and sing for joy."

SNACK

Plan a meal or snack that includes some of the Octoberfest foods: bratwurst, sauerkraut, pretzels, beer.

ENTERTAINMENT

I Picked A . . . Game. One player begins by saying "I picked a (and names a fruit or vegetable). The next player has to name a fruit or vegetable that starts with the same letter that the previous name ended with. Try to include as many fruits and vegetables that are brought to mind at harvest time as possible.

SHARING

1. Share what you like most about the fall season.
2. Share your favorite fruit and favorite vegetable.
3. Share something that you want to praise and thank God for.

CLOSING PRAYER

—Suggested Prayer: An Indian Prayer

Let me Walk in Beauty, and make my eyes ever behold the red and purple sunset.

Make my hands respect the things you have made and my ears sharp to hear your voice.

Make me wise so that I may understand the things you have taught my people.

Let me learn the lessons you have hidden in every leaf and rock.

I seek strength, not to be greater than my brother, but to fight my greatest enemy—myself.

Make me always ready to come to you with clean hands and straight eyes.

So when life fades, as the fading sunset, my spirit may come to you without shame.

(Indian Prayer from the Red Cloud Indian School, Pine Ridge, South Dakota)

CHEERING IN THE HARVEST

OPENING PRAYER

Generous Father, you have gifted us with the fruit of the land. As crops are harvested around the country we celebrate and thank you for them. Help us to be generous in sharing these gifts with our brothers and sisters around the world. *Amen.*

ACTIVITY TIME

Young Family

Gather fruits and vegetables from your refrigerator and cabinets and let everyone experience their shapes and smells. Then make popcorn in a way that the children can observe.

Middle Years Family

Play the Harvest Game. The first person begins by naming a fruit or vegetable or grain that is harvested. The next person repeats what has been said and adds one of his own, and so on. When a person misses, he is out of the game.

Adult Family

Read together Ecclesiastes 3:1-8, "There is an appointed time for . . ." Tell what it means to you and share with one another your times of planting and harvesting.

SNACK

Caramel apples and apple cider are seasonal favorites at this time of year.

ENTERTAINMENT

Pumpkin Seeds Race. Give each family member ten pumpkin seeds in a paper cup, along with a straw and a small dish. At the "go" signal everyone tries to pick up a seed and transfer it from the cup to the dish by sucking in on the straw. The first person to move all of his seeds wins. For older persons you can add more seeds or substitute an egg carton for the saucer and have the players drop a seed into each section.

SHARING

1. Share a time when you planted a seed and then had to wait for the harvest, like in a friendship or saving money for something, or learning a skill.
2. Share what comes to your mind when you see a bowl full of beautiful fruits and vegetables.
3. Share how you feel about waiting for anything.

CLOSING PRAYER

—Suggested Prayer: God our Father, you tend to our planting and our harvesting. Send your Spirit to help us care for and appreciate the gifts you have entrusted to us. *Amen.*

HOMECOMING

OPENING PRAYER

Lord Jesus, you came home to the Father when you paused to celebrate his love for you—in the desert when you prayed, on the mountain at the Transfiguration, and on that first Easter. Make us aware of our coming home to you and to one another when we come home from school, work, from a trip. Tonight we celebrate all those homecomings. *Amen.*

ACTIVITY TIME

Young Family

Plan a simple homecoming parade—decorate the wagon, tricycles, etc. Make crepe paper pom-poms; put together a band with kitchen utensils. Assign everyone a part—homecoming king and queen, attendants, band leader, etc.

If one of the family members is absent, a letter, tape or phone conversation could be included in the party.

You might also sit in a circle, campfire style. Share what you like most about coming home—after a day's work, after school, after a trip. Give cheers to each member of the family.

Middle Years Family

Depending upon the size of your family, have a backyard game—touch football, volleyball, badminton, croquet.

Then sit in a circle campfire style. Take turns role-playing different family members coming home. The rest of the family tries to guess who is being portrayed.

After the game, share your feelings about coming home, after a day's work, after school, after a trip.

Adult Family

Read together the story of the Prodigal Son (Luke 15:11-32). Discuss how your family comes home to one another. Think of ways to improve your homecoming events, recognizing them as very special times.

Design a welcome symbol for your entrance that expresses a warm welcome home. This might be a floor mat (a plain rubber mat can be decorated with marking pens) or a door hanging with symbols of peace, love and joy.

SNACK

Pumpkins are in season now. Find a recipe for pumpkin cookies, pumpkin pie, pumpkin bread.

ENTERTAINMENT

Fill a jar with seeds. Use the pumpkin seeds if you had fresh pumpkin for your snacks. Have a guessing contest. Then count the seeds together to see who came the closest.

SHARING

1. Share how you feel when you come home and nobody is home.
2. Share a time when you were away from home for a long time and your feelings about getting home again.

CLOSING PRAYER

—Scripture Reading: Luke 24:50-53

—or: Thank you, Lord, for our family homecoming celebration tonight and especially for this family to come home to. Help us to always receive each other with open arms and open hearts. *Amen.*

SUNDAY MORNING

OPENING PRAYER

Risen Lord, you marked Sunday as a very special day, when you arose from the dead and raised the hopes of all men. We want to be Alleluia people, celebrating each Sunday in a special way. Send your Spirit to guide our planning this evening so that we may grow in your love and in family togetherness. *Amen.*

ACTIVITY TIME

Young Family

Materials: paper, crayons. Talk about Sunday as a family party day. What can your little ones do to contribute to the party? Include them in every way possible. Print "Alleluia" in large block letters. Let them decorate it with bright colors and pictures, to be hung on the wall on Sunday morning. Take it down and hang it up again only on Sunday to help the children recognize that Sunday is special.

Middle Years Family

Discuss what your family customs are relative to Sunday. How is Sunday special for your family? Think of some things you might do to build your family tradition or custom: going to church as a family, helping to plan the Sunday liturgy, planning breakfast or brunch, a family outing, a visit to grandparents. Make something for Sunday's breakfast like placemats, napkin holders; decorate napkins or a candle; create a centerpiece for the table.

Adult Family

Materials: index cards, pencils. Have each person write down what he would like the family to do on Sunday. Put each idea on separate cards. Collect the cards, read them, combine similar ideas. Discuss how each person's favorite way of celebrating Sunday can be integrated into a Family Celebration of Sunday.

SNACK

Try some pudding-wiches by mixing ½ cup of peanut butter with 1½ cups milk. Then beat in a package of any flavor instant pudding. Let stand 5 minutes. Then spread between two graham crackers to make a sandwich. Freeze about three hours.

ENTERTAINMENT

Have each person take a turn singing, humming or whistling a song. Do only the first few notes and let the others try to guess the song. Add additional notes until the song is guessed or until everyone "gives up."

SHARING

1. Share your favorite Sunday memory.
2. Share one thing about yourself you would like to change.
3. Share one thing about yourself that you like and don't want to change.

CLOSING PRAYER

—Suggested Prayer: Sing a simple version of "Alleluia"

—or: Compose a litany of praise and thanksgiving. Each one names something he wishes to praise and thank God for and everyone responds "We praise and thank you, Lord."

SPOOKS AND SAINTS

OPENING PRAYER

Father, at this time when children enjoy the customs of Halloween with its ghosts and goblins, masks and costumes, tricks and treats, help us to recognize who we really are, our unmasked selves. Send your Spirit to help us to be more like your Son Jesus. *Amen.*

ACTIVITY TIME

Young Family

Carve out a pumpkin and place a candle inside. Turn off the lights and set up the atmosphere for Halloween fun. Let the children dress up in their costumes and masks. Talk about the characters they are masquerading.

Middle Years Family

Find out something about the life of your patron saint. Share with other members of your family. Early Christian people began celebrating a holy day the evening before the feast. Talk about the meaning of Halloween as the eve of All Saints. Make stick puppets representing each of your patron saints.

Adult Family

Read Romans 12:2. Talk about the different kinds of masks we sometimes wear and why we wear them. Reminisce about the childhood fears you had, real and imaginary. Share the fears and phobias you may have yet today. Make suggestions to each other as to how they might be dispelled or diminished.

SNACK

Make pumpkin faces on cupcakes or ice cream balls or decorate to resemble black cats, witches or goblins with licorice, candy corn, gumdrops, raisins, chocolate chips or sprinkles.

ENTERTAINMENT

Divide the family into two teams and play "Witches Relay." Give the first in line a broom and a pair of rolled socks. Each player sweeps the socks to the finish line and back and then hands the broom to the next player. The first team to finish wins the game.

SHARING

1. Share a time when you were really frightened.
2. Share the saint whom you would most like to be like.
3. Share why you like being yourself, most of all.

CLOSING PRAYER

—Suggested Prayer: Spontaneous Litany of Saints. A saint's name is mentioned and everyone responds, "pray for us."

THE GROWING STICK

OPENING PRAYER

Dear Father, tonight we are going to celebrate the wonder of our growth. We praise you for the gift of life and your nourishment that has helped us to grow. *Amen.*

ACTIVITY TIME

Young Family

This evening the family is invited to stand back and look at and celebrate the growth and development of each family member.

Bring out the baby books, pictures, baby shoes, other memorabilia. Share with the child the events that surrounded his birth, Baptism, early years up to the present time. If you do not have a memorabilia box you might make one so that items related to his growing can be displayed in his bedroom, on his wall or on a shelf. You might begin a tape recording of the child's voice which can be added to periodically.

Middle Years and Adult Families

Arrange snapshots of the family members at various stages of growth on a large bulletin board or cardboard. Exchange names and find fitting descriptions, humorous captions from magazines to be put under each picture.

SNACK

Hot apple cider, garnished with a stick of cinnamon.

ENTERTAINMENT

Variations of the Tag Game can be fun. "Shadow Tag" must be played at night. Try to step on someone's shadow if you are playing outside near a porch light. Or try to catch someone with a beam of light if you are using a flashlight.

SHARING

1. Share one sign or indication that you are growing in some way, physically, intellectually, etc.
2. Share a positive thought about how another family member has grown recently.

CLOSING PRAYER

—Scripture Reading: Romans 8:18-23

—or: Compose a family litany. "For the power I have to . . ."
All answer: "We praise and thank you, Lord."

ROOTS

OPENING PRAYER

Father, be present with us as we come to celebrate our family heritage. We recognize our rich ancestry in our family and in our church. We thank you for our parents, grandparents, and all those who have contributed to our family. *Amen.*

ACTIVITY TIME

Young and Middle Years Families

Place a tree branch in a can held in place with sand to represent your family tree. Decorate the tree stand and tree. Let the children hang pictures, snapshots or original illustrations of each family member on the tree. Go as far back into your heritage as your information permits.

Adult Family

Make a scrapbook of all the items you have that tell something about your past—valentines collected from grandparents, awards and achievements of family members, souvenirs, etc.

Photo Albums. Many families have pictures scattered here and there. Gather them together and decide on a meaningful arrangement and organize into your family photo album, which can serve as a record of your family's history. It will become more valuable with each passing year.

Design your own family Coat-of-Arms. It can be as simple or as elaborate as you choose—anything from paper and pencil, cardboard, wood, paints. The completed product should express the uniqueness that your family is—what you believe and value, what your family name means, where you came from, etc.

Tape Recordings—with cassette tape recorders found in so many homes today you can have an audio rather than only a written record of family events. Prepare a beginning entry to be recorded that tells all that you have found out about your ancestors. Add to it as new information appears.

SNACK

Popcorn or popcorn balls.

ENTERTAINMENT

Play "Did I ever Tell You?" by letting each person tell a story beginning with the words, "Did I ever tell you about the time when. . . ?"

SHARING

1. Share why you are happy and proud to be a member of this family.
2. Share your happiest family memory.
3. Share what you would like to be remembered for in the future family history.

CLOSING PRAYER

—Suggested Prayer: Father, all of us have our roots in you, who have given us life. Help us to treasure that life and appreciate those who have given us our family name and heritage. *Amen.*

THANKSGIVING

OPENING PRAYER

Loving Father, how grateful we are for all that you have so generously blessed us with. How can we begin to name them all and to thank you enough for every single gift? Know that we are appreciative and hope to grow even more so in the future. *Amen.*

ACTIVITY TIME

Young Family

Tell the Thanksgiving Story to your children or let the older children in the family tell it to the younger ones. Act it out letting the little ones have parts to play.

Middle Years Family

Write a family prayer of thanksgiving which includes all the specific things you want to thank God for. Print this on a large sheet of paper, with illustrations and decorations. Hang it on the wall where Thanksgiving dinner will be served and pray it together at dinner time.

Adult Family

Make preparations for the Thanksgiving table. Create a centerpiece that is symbolic of your family's gratitude and uniqueness.

Read Acts of the Apostles 2:46,47. Talk about how the family Thanksgiving meal is like the Church's celebration of the Eucharist. What similarities can you name?

SNACK

Mayflower Boats. Fill a peach or pear half with cream cheese. For a sail, poke a toothpick through a carrot shaving or a lemon or orange peel and stick it in the peach.

ENTERTAINMENT

See how many words you can make using only the letters in "Thanksgiving."

SHARING

1. Share the greatest blessing you have ever received.
2. Share the best way you can think of thanking God.
3. Share how you feel when someone gives you something and compare it with how you feel when you are the giver.

CLOSING PRAYER

If you composed a Family Prayer of Thanksgiving during *Family Night* activities, use that prayer to close the evening

—or: Thanksgiving for God's Blessings as expressed in Psalm 65.

Dear Friends in Christ:

Something marvelous and magnificent is in the bluster of the north winds and is dancing in the sparkling stars these chilly evenings.

Advent is beckoning to us, holding within itself the "Promise of Love" that is waiting to flower forth on Christmas Eve. Let us pause and be still so the whispers of Advent can reach our ears and touch our hearts with their message—PREPARE.

This year make Advent a special family time. As a family, enter these pages and enjoy Advent and Christmastime together. Take time to pray, to listen, to play and to love one another. Let the greatest gift we give one another this year be "time together." Time and love go hand-in-hand.

Happy Family Nighting!
The Reilly Family
and the Burbach Family

1st WEEK OF ADVENT

Theme: Anticipation

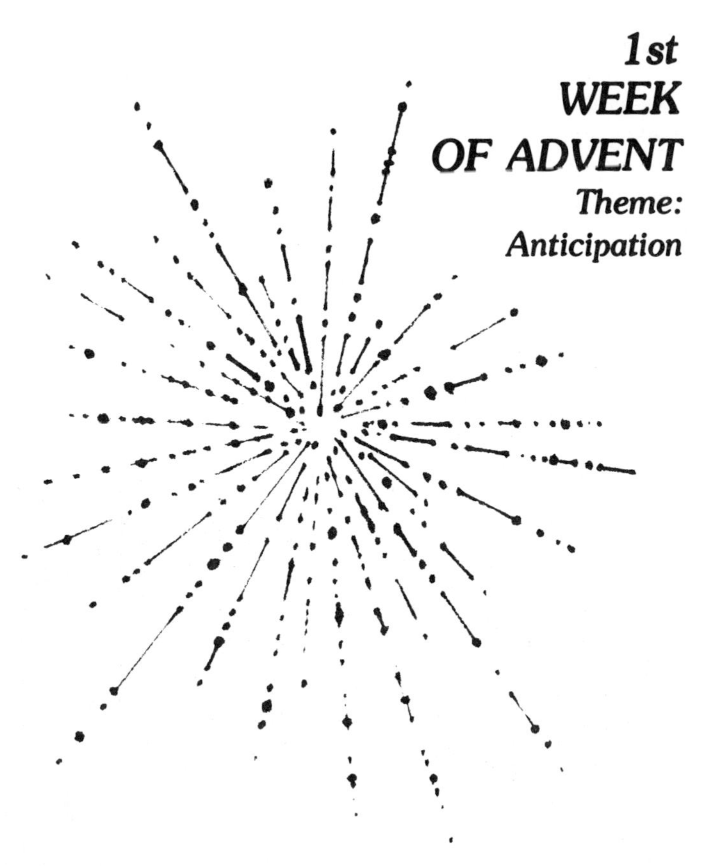

OPENING PRAYER

Dearest Lord, thank you for the beauty and joy of this first *Family Night* in Advent. Bless us as we gather together in your name, Oh Lord, to share, to grow and to love. Help us to make this Advent a time to prepare more than we ever have before for the coming of "Emmanuel." *Amen.*

ACTIVITY TIME

The Advent wreath is a lovely custom that helps the family to express visibly the meaning of this season of waiting and anticipation. It may be used all during Advent at mealtimes.

Materials: three purple candles, one pink candle (or four white candles can be used by tying purple bows on three and a pink bow on the fourth), four candleholders, live or plastic greens, wire or string, purple ribbon. Make a square with the four candles in the holders. With wire wind the greens around the candles to form a circle, decorate with a large purple bow. For fresh greens, a round jello mold filled with water will help them stay alive longer; as the season progresses, fresh greens can be added. When the wreath is completed try sharing these questions together: (a) why candles? (to symbolize Jesus as the Light of the World) (b) why evergreens? (God never changes, new life) (c) why the circle? (God is eternal, God has no beginning or end) (d) why the colors? (purple—a time to prepare, pink—the joy of Christmas is near). Try even more. Wonderful ideas can pop out of family members.

During the Advent season light a new candle each week. The third week light the pink one. Each week plan to sing "O Come, O Come Emmanuel" and read the following scriptures:

1st week: 1 Thes 5:19-24
2nd week: 1 Thes 3:11-13
3rd week: James 5:7-11
4th week: Phil 4:4-7

When Christmas Day arrives the candles may be changed to white and the greens decorated with little ornaments from the Christmas tree. Enjoy it nightly until January 6th known by tradition as "12th Night."

SNACK

Try some hot spiced tea, stirred with a cinnamon stick, and warm donuts.

ENTERTAINMENT

Play a game of charades with family members acting out special Christmas characters.

SHARING

Gather in a circle and take turns sharing:

1. When each family member felt especially joyful during the past week.
2. When someone felt close to God.
3. When someone felt loved by another family member.

CLOSING PRAYER

—Suggested Prayer: Gentle Lord, thank you for this evening together and for your presence in our midst. Bless each of us this coming week, Lord, and help us to reach out in kindness to all we meet. *Amen.*

2nd WEEK OF ADVENT

Theme: Concern for Others

OPENING PRAYER

Holy Spirit, prepare our minds and hearts during this Advent season. Make us open to each other. Let us reach out in love to bear each other's burdens as well as joys. Bless us, Holy Spirit, as we share this special *Family Night* together and hear our prayer for those who are lonely or unloved this holy season. *Amen.*

ACTIVITY TIME

What makes Advent and Christmas so joyous is sharing it with others: friends, relatives, neighbors, the poor and the lonely. Together, share some thoughts on why we are happy when we are thinking of and doing for others. Then choose one or more of the activity ideas below:

1. Handmade Christmas Cards. *Materials:* construction paper, crayons or magic markers, paste, scissors, friends' addresses, magazines. Go over the family Christmas card list and choose some names to mail handmade cards to. Share some thoughts on why the family sends cards and who they receive cards from. See how many different types of cards the family can make. Write a new message on each card. They can be folded in a three-section fold, glued shut, the address placed on the back side and mailed to those extra dear friends.

2. Advent Joy Kit. Choose an elderly person or someone who is alone or ill to present an Advent Joy Kit to. *Materials:* red construction paper, small inexpensive gifts (comb, nail file, playing cards), wrapping paper, ribbon, tape, small bits of writing paper. Make a large stocking out of the red paper and staple or tape it together. Decorate it. Be sure to mark it "Advent Joy Kit." Wrap a gift for each day until Christmas. Some can be little handwritten notes with scripture sayings or notes of cheer; others, little handmade or purchased gifts. Plan to deliver the stocking as a family on a Sunday afternoon or early on a weekday evening.

ENTERTAINMENT

Take a drive around town to look at all the Christmas lights and house decorations.

SNACK

Hot chocolate and popcorn balls.

SHARING

1. Each share an extra wonderful memory from a past Christmas.
2. Each make a wish for this Christmas.
3. Share a moment someone felt close to God recently.

CLOSING PRAYER

—Suggested Prayer: Oh God, our Father, thank you for this evening. We are waiting for your Son to come to us. Help us to see him when he comes to us in the love of our families, in the words of our priests or ministers and in all we meet this coming week. Come, Lord Jesus, come! *Amen.*

Read together Matt 2:6 and follow it by singing, "O Come, O Come Emmanuel."

3rd WEEK OF ADVENT

Theme: The Light of the World

OPENING PRAYER

Christ, Light of the World,
Shine above me,
Shine below me,
Shine around me.

Christ, Light of the World,
Sparkle within me,
Dance within me,
Speak within me,
Command within me.

Christ, Light of the World,
Take me, mold me,
Use me, hold me,
For I love you, Lord Jesus. *Amen.*

ACTIVITY TIME

This week the pink candle of joy on the family Advent wreath is lit to remind us Christmas Eve is drawing ever nearer. Tonight may be used to reflect back over Advent thus far and plan what still needs to be done to prepare for Christmas.

Choose one or more of the following:

1. The Joy Tree. *Materials:* small table size tree or large vase of greens, pens, pieces of paper 2 inches by 4 inches, red and green yarn or ribbon. Each family member fills a couple cards with a short prayer of praise or thanksgiving to God for blessings in the family or for friends during this Advent. The little Joy Notes may be hung on the tree with the colored yarn or ribbon. Place the tree in a prominent place along with new cards, yarn, and pens so that the family and friends may continue to place note prayers on the tree up until Christmas Eve. December 24th, collect them all together and wrap them as a gift for the Baby Jesus to be opened on Christmas Eve.

2. Birthday Box for Jesus. *Materials:* one good-size box, a Bible, wrapping paper, ribbon, tape, writing paper, pen. Place the Bible in the box with a marker set at Luke 2:1-20, "The Christmas Narrative." Then write a family letter to Jesus (say anything in your hearts, a welcome, whatever anyone wishes). Place the letter and Bible in the box. Wrap the box and place it under the tree to be opened and shared on Christmas Eve.

3. Bake Time. Together make homemade Christmas cookies or candies.

SNACK

Eggnog and homemade gingerbread boys.

ENTERTAINMENT

String popcorn and cranberries to use as decoration for the Christmas tree or wrap gifts for friends or relatives.

SHARING

1. Take turns finishing this sentence: Christmas is . . .
2. Mom and Dad share their favorite Christmas as a child.
3. Each share a joy or a struggle from the past week.

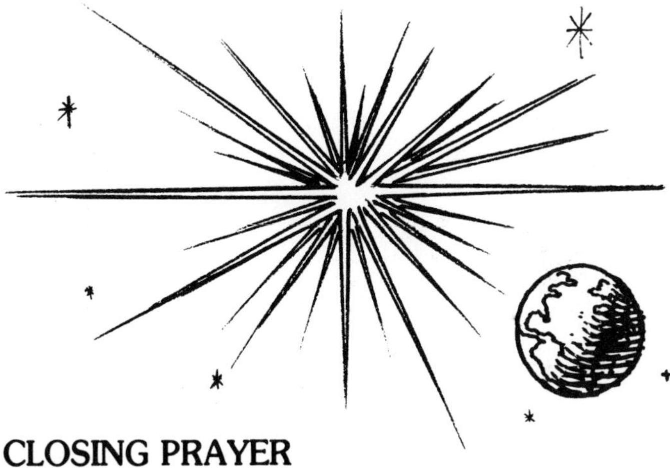

CLOSING PRAYER

—Suggested Prayer: Oh Wondrous and Gentle Lord, thank you for the beauties of this evening. How grateful our family is to you for the precious mysteries of Advent and Christmas. Help us to continue to prepare our hearts and minds for the holiness and awe of Christmas. Gentle Lord, remember those who are alone or unhappy. Help our family to reach out in love to all we meet this coming week. *Amen.*

4th WEEK OF ADVENT

Theme: Gifts for Jesus

OPENING PRAYER

Dearest Lord, bless us as we come together tonight as a family in joyful anticipation of your birthday. Fill us, O Lord, with the brotherhood of all peoples and help us to share our family's love with the lonely, the poor and your people everywhere. *Amen.*

ACTIVITY TIME

Manger Time. *Materials:* one large white sheet, manger figures (if the family doesn't have a set, the figures can be cut out of cardboard and colored with crayons). The birth of the Baby Jesus is only a few nights away. If the tree is not up yet, now would be a good time for the family to put it up together. If it's already up, remove all the presents so its base is empty. The lights may be lit, the room darkened. Take turns sharing what the tree symbolizes to me.

(In Germany during the 1600's people used to hang apples and white wafers on trees to symbolize the Holy Eucharist. Thus, the tree

that had borne the fruit of sin for Adam and Eve now bears the saving fruit of the Eucharist symbolized by the wafers. Later these wafers were made into stars, hearts, flowers and bells which have evolved into our present day decorations.)

Now pass out a manger character to each family member (larger families—one figure for two people). Ask each to share what that character of the Christmas story gave because he loved (example: Joseph—a home for Jesus). Then each take a turn sharing what he or she may give out of love for Jesus. Place the white sheet under the tree and place all the manger figures, except the Baby Jesus, on the sheet near the manger or stable. Sing together, "O Come, O Come Emmanuel."

SNACK

Cranberry punch and homemade cookies.

ENTERTAINMENT

Plan to go out around the neighborhood caroling as a family. Come home to another treat—this time, hot chocolate.

SHARING

1. Share a memory of a favorite Christmas tree from the past.
2. Share what each would like to do to make this Christmas Eve more enchanting.
3. Share when someone felt especially happy the past couple of days.

CLOSING PRAYER

—Suggested Prayer: Oh, God, thank you for this evening and the warmth and joy we feel this Christmas season. How grateful we are at Jesus' birthday soon to come. Be with us, Lord, in our final preparations for this great day. *Amen.*

CHRISTMAS EVE SUGGESTIONS

1. Plan a birthday party for the Baby Jesus. Have a birthday cake, napkins, balloons and be sure to sing "Happy Birthday" to Jesus.

2. Turn off all the lights in the house except the tree lights. Each family member carry a small lit candle and choose someone to carry the Baby Jesus. Have a procession all through the house singing "Silent Night." Then place Jesus in the manger under the tree. Christmas morning, presents can go under the tree.

3. Darken the house and light one candle. Read aloud the Christmas story from Luke 2:1-20 and sing carols.

4. Burn a candle in the front window of the house and stay up until it burns out on its own. Started in Ireland many years ago, this custom is a welcome to the Christ Child.

FAMILY FUN IDEAS FOR CHRISTMAS WEEK

Sometimes Christmas week is a big letdown after all the excitement of Advent and Christmas Day. Try some of these ideas to perk up droopy spirits.

1. Hold a dinner one evening on the floor around the Christmas tree. Use plastic place mats or a plastic tablecloth.

2. Plan a pot luck supper for a couple of neighborhood families.

3. Celebrate the 12 days of Christmas by giving little gifts to family members each day (25c to 50c is plenty).

4. Bake Day. Bake family favorites—breads, cookies, candies and then plan to take some to a few friends as a "New Year's Surprise."

5. Hold a game fest: monopoly, bridge, the ungame.

6. Hold a story period at a set time and read aloud to the children a book from the library—of course, that means a fun trip to the library to pick out some special books by the family.